Orkidedatter

A Fire Eyes Erotic Fantasy

Volume 1

JAMES MUSGRAVE

With Lily Orkidedatter

DEDICATION

To all people who've suffered from childhood abuse and neglect. Please contact authorities (teachers, doctors, police) and be honest about what happened to you. Shame is what makes us resist reaching out. Unless we can be honest about these issues, they will remain the worst hidden epidemic in human history.

CONTENTS

ACKNOWLEDGMENTS

We want to acknowledge our families and their support after childhood traumas. We also support RAINN and will donate proceeds to continue the work of these fine people to assist abused individuals. Our wonderful cover artist A. R. Mirabal made developing this novel a pleasurable experience.

Other Works by This Author

The Pat O'Malley Series
Forevermore: A Pat O'Malley Historical Mystery
Disappearance at Mount Sinai: A Pat O'Malley Historical Mystery
Jane the Grabber: A Pat O'Malley Steampunk Mystery
Steam City Pirates: A Pat O'Malley Steampunk Mystery

The Digital Scribe: A Writer's Guide to Electronic Media
Lucifer's Wedding
Sins of Darkness
Russian Wolves
Iron Maiden an Alternate History
Love Zombies of San Diego
Freak Story: 1967-1969
The President's Parasite and Other Stories
The Mayan Magician and Other Stories
Catalina Ghost Stories

Portia of the Pacific Historical Mystery Series
The Spiritualist Murders
The Stockton Insane Asylum Murder
Portia of the Pacific Historical Mystery Trilogy

"If thou rememb'rest not the slightest folly
That ever love did make thee run into,
Thou has not loved."

– *As You Like It*, Act 2, scene 3, lines 33 – 35

NORSE FAMILY TREE

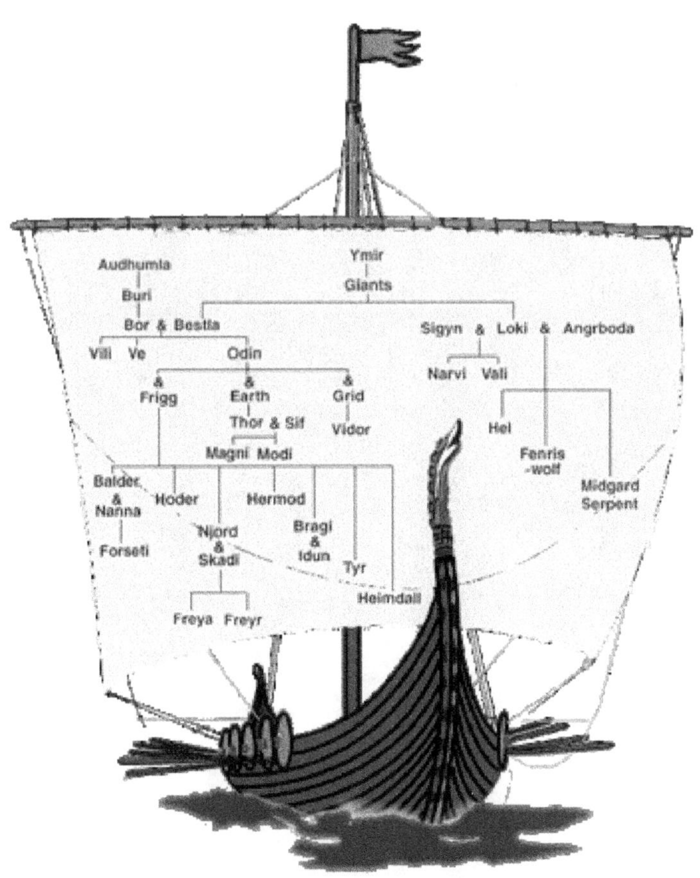

CHAPTER ONE: IS THAT ALL THERE IS?

September 2022, Oslo, Norway.

I finally find out some of what Lily does when she's inside her cabin in the woods. She watches re-runs of *Charlie's Angels*. You know. That old show where the gorgeous "angels" spy and do other deeds of daring for their "old man," Charlie, the wealthy guy who always makes remarks that keep his girls motivated. When she tells me this, just before we begin our work to shut down Dr. Balder's Valhalla sex trafficking castle forever, I say this:

"You really disappoint me, Lily. You're college educated and a psychotherapist. If that program were *Chekhov's Angels*, or even the *Marquis de Sade's Angels*, I might believe it. After what happened yesterday, I think I'm the one who needs psychotherapy."

I am relieved that she's back to the land of the talking dead, and she's even smiling again with blue eyes, not red. But the threads of real-world horror and our Gothic land of erotic Norse Folklore are ensnarling us in a final battle with forces I don't want to meet. And, quite frankly, I don't want Lily to meet them either. She's been sexually addicted only to the creatures Balder has sent to seduce her. Lily no longer knows how to love a human. What if this mad wizard does it again before she can overtake the castle?

While Lily watches her Charlie girls for thirty-minutes last night, I'm inside The Thief Hotel watching a three-hour movie based on my favorite author Haruki Murakami's fiction. The name of the film, *Drive My Car*, as a matter of fact, is kind of nightmarish, considering my eighty-six-year-old Uber driver's trip around the Norway mountain curves, but that's beside the point. I taught literature, and Lily didn't. However, I do want to quote one passage from the Murakami story because it just about sums up my philosophy of life and what I must face with my partner:

> *The proposition that we can look into another person's heart with perfect clarity strikes me as a fool's game. I don't care how well we think we should understand them, or how much we can love them. All it can do is cause us pain. Examining your own heart, however, is another matter. I think it's possible to see what's in there if you work hard enough at it. So in the end maybe that's the challenge: to look inside your own heart as perceptively and seriously as you can, and to make peace with what you find there. If we hope to truly see another person, we have to start by looking within ourselves.*

So, I begin to follow that wisdom from fiction, as I begin to see the entire world as a fiction. After watching that fantastic film, I now look inside myself and find that I am not a psychologist, or even a decent criminologist, but Lily is. And, most specifically, I know little to nothing about how she gets her powers over me or anything else in her supernatural life.

I am human, and I love her. This has meant nothing to her. There's only the magic world of her Norse folklore and the wizardry of Dr. Balder and his spirit son, Loki. They must meet to determine the result. I know that she holds all the cards in our deck right now, and I am only along for the ride to lend her any assistance I can.

"Orkidedatter, listen to me. Will you? All I know for certain is what I can see, hear, taste, smell, and touch. You've already messed my mind out of at least four out of five of my senses, although you also know what I already said about that weirdest of all our senses, sight. Before we go any further in this case, I want you to explain the following things that I believe you know. Is that okay with you, my dear? Before you turn me into a troll or some other creature from your creature kit?"

She still has that grin on her face. It's so repugnant to the character I've known all these months, that I begin to get hot. Not with my usual lust for her body, or for her poetry, but pissed at her god-awful smile, at this moment in time, when everything—possibly even the fate of the planet—is on the line.

As she steps down off the front porch of her cabin, I half-expect her to grow bat wings again and fly around naked, but she doesn't. She strides up to me, takes me by my hands, and stares into my eyes. Is she trying to hypnotize me? Put me into a trance because I witnessed her murder Hodr, the bi-sexual lover boy of the Norway Underworld? Jesus!

"Martin, don't be afraid. I know you've been fearful for quite some time. I was that way until I wrote that poem about Marilyn Southbine, the child who murdered her uncle. She unlocked doors that I never realized existed. I knew I was a medium, for example, and that I could communicate with the dead, but these supernatural connections happened without my control. In fact, I asked you to come to Norway because I sensed you were an important ingredient to stop Dr. Balder."

"Ingredient? What are you making? An apple pie?" I pull her to me and hug her. I can feel her breasts against my chest. "Lily, please tell me what is real and what is imagined. Or I swear, I am going to go stark, raving mad, until I know what's happening. That serial killer, Ingunn Dahl, for example. What threat is she? Does she have a physical body? Who can you control and who can you harm? Can you use your creature forms against real people?"

Lily breaks away from my grip. Her smile is gone. She looks up at the sun over the waving trees.

"My mother's spirit told me last night that the girl, Marilyn, and her mother, Olga, have been killed. She saw it happen inside one of the rooms in Balder's castle. He called upon Ingunn Dahl to help him murder them."

"*Ah herregud*!" I exclaim. It's the only Norwegian I've picked up during these months in Oslo. "You didn't answer my question. How can you fight back and what can we use?"

Her gaze meets mine again. "Interpol called me. They are also going to be at the castle along with our local police. What happened yesterday was real. We need to first find the mistletoe bush to construct the arrow needed to kill Baldr, which is Dr. Balder's spirit identity. This is how he gets his power. The evil spirit of his son, Loki, manifested itself after he was murdered by Anders Breivik on 22 July 2011. When Balder built the Valhalla Castle, Loki was helping him construct the worldwide sex trafficking business being run in the center part of the fortress section. It's called the Circle of Maldoror."

"Center part? Maldoror? I don't understand. What does this have to do with your Norse legend and the end of the world?" My voice is getting dry, and my heart is thumping in my chest. I've never had heart trouble, so this is not the time to start having it.

"Mother says she was working for Loki, but now she's returned to help us. Loki worships the text of the French poet, Lautréamont's *Les Chants de Maldoror*. They've created rooms where many different lurid acts can be created and sold to rich and powerful people who want to visit. They can also protect these people's identities so as not to duplicate the mistakes made by other traffickers such as Jeffrey Epstein in your country. However, the main purpose is to record these activities so they can blackmail these wealthy leaders and gradually take-over the world."

"Wait a minute. Take over *this* world? What about the world of your ancestors? You know. The last battle of Ragnarök. Will this happen if you kill Hodr's brother, Dr. Balder?"

I watch Lily transform in front of me into the form of Hela again. Her wide bat wings, the dark armor, and bearskin. She snarls at me, shows her canines and black forked tongue before leaping into the air, her wings beating so violently that I feel the wind against my face. She looks down at me and her mouth opens.

"Stay here until I return! I must first find the mistletoe bush. We will then leave to murder Balder at his castle."

I watch her rise higher, above the trees, as she flies off toward the distant mountains of Rondane. I decide this is the time to do some spying of my own. She must have something inside her cabin that can help me understand who she *really* is and what I've gotten myself into.

Believe it or not, I get inside the cabin with my credit card. Lily needs a bolt lock, but with her powers, perhaps the outside needs to keep her inside. The place is very Spartan. A military green cot with a pillow and blanket. No furniture. One front window. A hotplate and no refrigerator. Wait. There's a book under her bed. I take it out, sit down on the cot and open it up. It's a journal. So, she does write more than just poetry on the toilet. This goes way back. It's a diary. Her different foster care homes in Oslo. Basic things about school gossip, who is telling secrets about whom. Here's something interesting. It's when she first saw the fox at the window on her grandfather's farm. She's writing it in her child's voice, so she must be five or six years old. I run the Norwegian through my cell phone's translator:

Dear Diary, Grandpa's woman is behind him when he show the dead fox to me. I can see threw her. She burn my head with her point finger! I can think strange thoughts now. I can move things. I can see smoky people all around. What are they?

What can that mean? That dead prostitute must be a ghost? Maybe she puts a curse on Lily? Or maybe she's giving her a gift to protect herself from her grandfather, the murderer? I must get out of here before Lily comes back.

My partner flies back down in front of the cabin about fifteen minutes after I exit it. She has the mistletoe arrow in her hand to kill Dr. Balder, and she's back inside her powder blue business suit.

"What? You're not going to go as Hela to the castle?" I ask, thinking about the irony of this murder weapon in Norse folklore being what we in the West use to get a free kiss at Christmas parties. I suppose it fits, as mistletoe is a parasitic plant that can kill trees left to its own devices. Great plant for Lily's murder weapon.

"No. Things have become a lot worse than before. There is a war on now. Putin has his Chechen soldiers outside, guarding the castle, and Dr. Balder has his monsters, inside, guarding Loki's Circle of Maldoror."

If I were chewing some gum, I would have swallowed it. "What can we do? Can the police or Interpol do anything to these creatures inside the castle?"

"No, but my creatures can," Lily turns her back to me and looks out toward the woods. She then blasts out a shriek I didn't know she had inside her, as a human, a Hela, or a Huldra. After several minutes, I feel the ground shaking, and then the trees begin to part in front of the cabin. Perhaps two hundred Huldrekall warriors from beneath the earth come marching up to us, along with the same number of female Huldras.

As we both gaze out at these monsters, waiting to do Lily's will, she turns to me and smiles, and I get another quick glimpse into her heart, when she tells me, "You know, Martin. I really wish I could be Catwoman. I don't like all this macho power. I like sneaking around."

That's my Lily.

I get the idea when we're preparing to leave. Anyhow, I think it's worth a shot. I figure perhaps Lily might be stuck in her ways a bit and hasn't realized what I told her about matter being forms and the ability she possesses to change them.

"Hey, Orkidedatter! Before you send off your little minions and turn me into a troll, have you thought that maybe you can become a catwoman, and that you can even cause your little monsters to behave like the cats you love so much? It makes sense, doesn't it? These are fascists we're going up against. During the Second World War, the Allies were able to get the upper hand on the Axis powers because they were too disciplined and tied to doing things in a ritual and orderly way, right?"

She turns to stare at me, a slightly quizzical look on her lovely face. "I suppose so, although that was then, and this is now."

I see my moment to pounce, and I seize it. "That's the point, goofy. Time is not real. I mean, what if people don't change much because of their conditioning, so they stay the same. So, they can be defeated using the same techniques that worked before, in earlier periods of fictitious history. Why do I say history is fiction? Think about it. History is written by the victorious, usually, right? And totalitarians believe in history so much that they order their followers to revolt against what they've determined are the evil class of folks, usually the rich and greedy or simply ones that they say subvert the masses' will."

"We need history to learn from, so we don't repeat the same mistakes," she responds.

"But what if this history is only what each person believes it is? How can one historian, or even a group of them, know what happens inside the minds of billions of humans each day, for thousands of years? What if history is not a collective truth that needs to be revolted against to survive but a relative fiction that each person invents to cope with the chaos all around us. I'm kind of playing off a few philosophers here, so bear with me."

"All right, Martin. I kind of like where you're going with this."

"We, the Allies, in World War Two, and in other wars, believe in the power of the individual so much that we're willing to take risks and improvise when our lives are at stake. Understand? So, you simply do this also. Improvise and become a cat woman. Improvise and give your minions the free will to sneak around and conquer by any means they think is necessary to achieve the goal."

"I see! Yes, you may be right." Lily turns to face her monsters. She waves her hands and chants some mumbo-jumbo that I am not aware she knows. Can it be the power that was given to her on the farm with her grandfather? Who knows? Her minions begin to react.

The Huldrekalls shuffle their giant feet and look at each other. They feel their own faces, their gigantic muscles, and their razor-sharp teeth inside the black ooze of their mouths, and when their black, forked tongues begin to swipe across their chests, they invent, and they swirl their tongues above their heads like lassos and play different versions of rope the other guy like a cowboy. Each one is unique in how he does this, and this is what I meant. Lily finally understands and is using her power to do this.

The Huldras do the same thing, only with their speedy and powerful legs, and their spiny backs. They leap and twist in the air, and crash against trees, their backs tearing apart the bark and splitting the timber into small pieces. They scream and collide into each other like romping children. It's a magnificent display of impromptu martial arts.

I feel proud of myself as I watch Lily change into her Norway version of the Catwoman. Unlike my Western commercial idea of this creature, which was made into probably the worst movie ever created, starring Halle Berry, Lily's version is much subtler and uniquely profound. Whereas DC Comics could never make up its collective minds about what kind of villain Catwoman should be to Batman, Lily immediately intuits that her Catwoman needs to be a product of her darkest experiences with actual serial killer women she's known and questioned. In fact, she tells me that she much prefers male serial killers, as they brag and describe their acts in a very straightforward way, whereas women are like "sneaky snakes," forever lying, twisting the facts, and never owning up to their evil and devious ways.

"I'm a villain to Dr. Balder, and he's a villain to me," she tells me, as she drives her Volvo onto the dirt road. We're heading back to Oslo and then on to Valhalla Castle on Utøya island. I guess I should describe her in detail, but I'm a bit chagrined in my present troll identity. She's given me braided red hair, a Santa Claus helper's suit, with a Robin Hood green hat, and a shiny-pink bulbous nose that resembles a clown rather than a man. I also have that same stooped, chubby posture that makes me look as if I'm eighty-seven rather than fifty-seven.

"You're starting to become a villain to me, Lily," I say, but I notice my voice is the same as my human voice. Thank goodness for small favors, I suppose. "How am I supposed to battle anybody looking the way I now do? Perhaps I can send them into conniption fits of laughter. Was that your plan for me?"

"You're a pacifist. I am trying to protect you, Martin. You mean very much to me. It is your brain I want to preserve. You seem to know how to proceed in our strategy, whereas I have the power to become the forms you described as being so flexible. I agree. My magical shapeshifting and powers over you and my creatures are natural to me. But we seem to be headed into something strangely fortuitous. It's almost as if it is predetermined by some curse or higher powers of predestination."

She turns toward me, her whiskers bouncing as she talks. She is more like a character in the Broadway musical *Cats* than from a Batman movie. I've not seen her in any of her other Norse creature forms, but this one is hardly sexy, unless cat beasts happen to be your libidinous pleasure.

She is as large as a human, but her torso is furry orange, like a Tabby, with a front chest of fluffy-cotton white, that, I see has no breasts and goes down between her legs like a snow drift. She seems to handle her clawed paws okay, on both ends, to drive a car, even a clutch like her Volvo. However, I keep staring at her perky ears and twinkling blue eyes and picturing that old *Saturday Night Live* routine of "Toonces the Driving Cat." At the end of each episode the cat, of course, ends up crashing the car, along with her human companions. I don't want to mention it, as "Toonces and the old

Troll" might even make Lily laugh. We're supposed to be on a serious mission.

"What powers do you have now, Lily? I know your Huldras and Huldrekalls are finding the way to the castle on their own right now, but what can you do when we get there? You already told me he's Baldr, the son of Odin, in your Norse legend, and he has the same powers to send out and occupy creatures as you do. And his son, Loki, is the same evil Loki."

Her voice sounds like a purr. "I cannot make love to a human right now, even in my human form. Dr. Balder took over my mother's spirit, and he also controls my sexual fantasy life. When mother returned, she told me about how Balder also controls my doppelganger, the serial killer, Ingunn Dahl. They murdered the two Huldras sent by me to infiltrate his castle. The world is turning to darkness and evil unless we stop them. That is in our Norse legend."

I stare at the winding road in front of us. I must give her the only wisdom I've learned through my personal life and with my experiences in the fabricated war in Iraq.

"Lily, there is only a razor's edge between saints and sinners in this world. Animals and monsters behave through their DNA and instinctual conditioning They stop before wholesale slaughter. We behave because we can make a choice with our brain. We can slaughter millions based on national and religious pride. What do you think will be our choice from now on? Or do you even know?"

"The truth, Martin, is like a dream. I saw it unfold after my last rendezvous with the white Huldrekall sent by Dr. Balder. I did research into my culture, as I was never educated about it, and I seem to be channeling the powers of the Vanir, which were the second group of mostly female gods in the Norse pantheon, who fought with the first group, the Aeser. The Vanir could see the future, and many were witches."

"Yes. I know this. So, are you fighting the Aeser for domination?" I scratch my bulbous nose.

"Not exactly. That war already took place. It united the two groups into one pantheon. I believe what's happening now is a turf war for power. Perhaps even the ultimate power over the world's future." Lily shows her canines in a cat smile or yawn. "Let me tell you where it stands based on our legend."

"All right. It's always nice to know which side you're on," I smile back at her.

"Deep in the forests of Jötunheim stood the hall of Angrboda. It was here that the giantess gave birth to three children of Loki: Finrir, Jörmungandr, and Hel. Fenrir was born a wolf cub. Jörmungandr was born as a snake, and Hel was born half dead."

"Also, please tell me the humans who figure into this legend. I already know about Balder as the son of Odin, and now Loki." I am fascinated, as this can be what our future will entail since Lily's already admitted she's initially from the magical pantheon of the Vanir. Except we don't know how that happened or who she is.

"I was already the form of Hel. In my lucid dream, or spiritual rendezvous, you were with me. So, you are now part of this magic. I had sex with the blind son of Odin, Prince Hodr, so I suppose he is in league with Dr. Balder as well." She turns onto the paved road that goes to Oslo.

"All right. The wolf, the snake, and you, Hel, as the Goddess of the Underworld. What else about this legend?"

"For a brief time, they lived in their mother, the giantess's hall on Jötunheim and were left in peace. But the Aeser discovered their existence, along with a prophecy that these three would bring doom to them during Ragnarök, the end of the world. It was then that Loki's children were declared to be monsters. Odin made the decision, but of course Odin dies at the end of the world when Fenrir the Wolf kills him. Only Odin's quiet son, Vidar, can save the day and kill the wolf."

"Where are we in the real world? What happens today at Balder's Valhalla Castle?" Boy, do my Troll underarms sweat! I hope Lily's pussycat smell doesn't pick up on my odor.

"As far as I can determine, Dr. Balder can control the white Haldrekall, but no others, the serial killer, Dahl, and perhaps Hodr, Baldr's blind brother. But the legend is legend. We don't know how it will take place now. The variables are almost limitless. What about Putin's Chechen guards, and all the other human contacts Dr. Balder and his Titan Energy company has? If I can't love humans, then Dr. Balder may even control me, at the deepest psychological level possible!"

CHAPTER TWO: IN THE BEGINNING

February 2022, Oslo, Norway.

I am Astrid's mother, Ingrid, and I haunt my daughter, so she says, but I prefer to call myself her protector, or perhaps in my lighter moments, her guardian angel. Or, perhaps more succinctly, I can be termed by the Norse folklore as a "mara ghost," who sits on your chest and brings you the nightmares. No! The only nightmares my daughter has she brings on herself. Such as this dream, she has now, about which I am now going to explain.

Astrid "Lily" Orkidedatter begins to have the dream right after she works on the case about the little girl who murders her uncle in his sleep and then slices him up, placing the perfectly shaped pieces of his corpse into different crevasses inside her toys.

An attractive woman, age thirty-eight, and five feet four inches tall, Lily wears a powder-blue business suit to work that fits her hourglass frame. Her intelligent eyes know how to pierce any criminal's ruse or any demon's facade. She also has rising, arched eyebrows, long blonde hair, a nymphet's smile, and a boisterous, Viking laugh.

The cabin is located on a shady plot of land she says is "between the trees and the mountains," and it's snowing hard. The poem's ink has yet to dry when she hears the creature's first echoing wail. It's as if the snow were torturing this being in some way. She says it's the same torture she's experiencing, having to interview the murderer child demon for the police.

She's used to hearing things, as she also does private work exorcizing ghosts from homes and speaking to the dead spirits of lonely relatives. I'd wager she wishes she could get rid of me. The discussion she has with the police is when she interviews Marilyn Southbine, the girl, about her killing her uncle. They're joking about how the girl should be "turned out" into the woods to become a Huldra.

"Sure, Lily, you take her and make some money. You can start the little whorehouse in the woods!" They laugh, in their gutter humor, and she has a half a mind to agree. This child is pure evil.

"Maybe she's not so pretty to be a Huldra. No tail either," she tells them, smirking. "Einar, maybe you should take her to your Huldrekall basement where you live with your mother. You could use her back to scrape slush off when you go inside." She's referencing wooden spikes that the Huldras supposedly have protruding from their naked backs. In all other respects, besides the fox tail, they're luscious, folklore femme fatales roaming the forests of Scandinavia and Germany.

In the cabin, Astrid looks down at the poem and reads it again, listening intently for perhaps some responsive answer to this horrific and masculine wail. Perhaps it's a call from her own troubled soul.

When she hears nothing, she decides to play the CD she owns of the American group called The Clovers from 1956. A retired poet, crime writer, and professor, Dr. Martin Seagraves, posts it on her Facebook newsfeed, and she burns it off YouTube. She smiles because Norway has a higher software piracy rate than the United States. The melody of "Devil or Angel" fills her cabin's confines with its spirited blues sound, as she reads over her poem once more:

☠ The Evil Lives Inside ☠

A devil's play, living a nightmare in her head, and with a mind of a monster talking to her. A little girl squeezing her teddy bear with blood dripping from her hands.

A difficult girl with no boundaries. A sweet girl with no rules. An angry girl with evil inside.

Her toys were in order and never played with. Her body was tightening up, shaking with an inferno in her eyes. Sitting like a guardian over her toys when she was crushing spiders to the floor.

Other people were cuddling her hair, but they were only checking her skull for a 666 sign. Did she perform as a clown at children's parties, using teeth from human skulls as a necklace? Rattling like a venom snake around her neck as a hypnotic melody?

A devil in disguise walking down the havoc line with a knife in her hand. A devil is unchained this cold night. Disrupting mess of a predator instinct, smiling at the silhouettes in the streetlights.

Blood runs cold in the dead of the night, when a little girl with emptiness in her eyes, was cutting his throat when he was asleep and resurrecting him into her deformed materials of a dark illusion.

She watched the blade covered with blood and took her killing to another level. She sliced him into pieces, the smell of fresh blood and meat was satisfying. A perfect square of human flesh like her toys. A dead man's body was a playground for a monster and when the butcher's knife cut a larger wound in his face, she was laughing out loud.

She licked the wound empty of blood.... took his eyeballs and chewed them as gum. From his skeleton she built a killer's castle and turned it into a macabre torture chamber.

Bloody footprints, a huge pool of blood, and a numb girl. She stands in the spotlight with a twisting tongue on the knife edge... blood on her lips and a mischievous smile on her face, like a China doll, with a horrific secret beneath unseen eyes.

She finds herself laughing after the last line. The police she works with laugh also. Sometimes, she knows, they're laughing *at* her, as I'm doing after hearing that abominable poem. They are, after all, police "scientists," and the world of spirits and demons makes no sense to them. However, when all other scientific resources are exhausted, when the victims and their families become outraged and start complaining to the media and to the mayor's office, she suddenly becomes "acceptable." In fact, without her interview of this child killer, as well her "conversation" with the dead spirit of this child's uncle, they have no clues about how to treat her mind and prevent future monsters like Marilyn.

However, in Lily's mind, she's thinking of this moment only. It's always "this moment" that terrifies her the most. She knows there's no real past or future in her world. Her own abuse demons always come back to haunt her consciousness. Her relatives who molested and beat her. Her nightmares of monsters, ghouls, and ghosts never disappear due to her post traumatic stress. I know I'm partly to blame for this. She was never able to have any kind of normal life. Never married, she's been an orphan of foster families her entire so-called "life."

Like a blonde, Norway version of Sarah Bernhardt, the Nineteenth Century French actress, whom she resembles, Lily, as she likes to call herself, Orkidedatter, is the unwed daughter, not of orchids, but of me, a prostitute named Ingrid, who worked in the center of Oslo. This area is where the officials keep watch and collect taxes when prostitution is legal.

Today, Lily knows, by name, most of these "sex workers," or even *hjelpepleier* health workers, as they like to be called. They can openly conduct their trade if the brothels or hotels are not charging anything or soliciting anywhere in the press or online. As her spirit mother, I am proud of her for doing this.

According to the press, the levels of prostitution profit have returned to over three hundred ninety million kroner or sixty-three million dollars per year, the same amount as before the 2009 laws were passed. Obviously, somebody's pulling some strings to keep the business thriving, and there are many "health spas and massage workers" advertising their legal services.

When the retired professor she meets online tells her he was raped at twelve years of age out on a California fishing jetty, by six men, her pointy, demon ears perk up immediately. She knows those sounds. He doesn't have to tell her. The grunting lust, boozy wheezes, drugged obsessions, profane curses, squishy flesh, and all the rest, are emblazoned in her memory forever.

Norway might have lower crime rates than in the States, overall, and has sentences of twenty-one years maximum for horrendous crimes, with no capital punishment, but police know about the demons of organized crime who also take advantage of this kind of legal weakness.

Lily works for the police, and she's stared at these monsters across the table for twenty years. She sees them in her dreams at night. The prostitutes, the pedophiles, and worst of all, the silent torturers of young bodies and minds, the ones who are closest to their children and who create the worst traumas. The familial incest beasts who, most always, get off without any punishment. The professor says these laws are the same way in the States.

These incest victims, she knows, become the prostitutes like me, her mother, strutting their "stuff" in the red-light districts of Oslo, and most of these child victims have some record of abuse in their past, even if not officially recorded. I, for example, am very educated, spending most of my off-hours inside the library or in the many museums in Oslo. The rape statistics, my daughter knows, are so low because of this, but the other side of the knife are the rapes of daughters, of sons, and of babies, hidden in the darkness of nurseries, under the pale light of the months of the tourist attraction called the "Midnight Sun," when the illusion of dawn meets the illusion of sundown. It becomes a twenty-four-hour horror show.

Lily only sees the bodies and ghosts of the battered victims, the maimed and the bloody, the tortured souls she knows will grow up to be deformed psyches and seekers of the shadowy underworld of crime and the real horror she witnesses every day. The liberal laws in Norway often let predators go free.

Like Hans Wortle, who believes he's a werewolf and stabs an Oslo prostitute forty-seven times. That working girl, by the way, is me, her mother. The medical psychologists give him antidepressants and counseling, and today he's teaching in Oslo schools, like Andrei Chikatilo (the Red Ripper serial killer) did in Russia!

Often, when my daughter wakes up shivering with night sweats, she wonders if she might also murder someone. Yes, she decides.

Given the right circumstances, it's going to happen one night, or day—possibly very soon.

"Your body, as you call it, comes from the illusion of the light shining upon your eyes, which, by the way, is processed by a brain that, when not functioning on its own, is worthless. Do you create your own thoughts? Or do thoughts create you?" That's what the old crime reporter and college professor tells her on messenger when she relates her dream.

In the dream, she's become that little girl she interviewed, and daughter Lily's boundaries have also fallen away. She begins to dance with the demons from her folklore, the nymphs, the tailed devils, and the monsters, like Grendel, within the many caves of the mountains, her country's dens of sensual promiscuity. She knows the pornographers use her idyllic scenery to shoot their lurid dreams, using these same abused women.

To the animals, killing is as natural as waking up to go to work in the morning. To soldiers at war, it's the same thing once they're conditioned. Do these dreams and thoughts create her, the murderer child, or can she fight back to control them? Her dream finally ends when the shadow figure of a giant appears in the forest outside her cabin.

The outlines of his muscles and shoulders, his huge head, the sound of his panting and demonic passion make her libido run wild, but her brain twists like a snake when she remembers this monster lives beneath us. She awakens, thrashing out at the midnight sun that pierces through her window.

Jeg elsker deg! The monster's masculine voice is shouting "I love you!"

The snow has stopped, and she knows something ominous is now afoot. She looks down at her body. Her business suit has been removed, and she's standing beside the military-style cot, where she sleeps, in her sports bra and *la Vie en Rose* white-laced panties.

I've undressed her, not wanting her to sleep in her clothes all night. The symbols of her years working with the police, her tattoos, radiate—almost glow—as the eternal light streams into the cabin from the front room's window. Her main tattoo, her namesake, the huge and delicately woven "orchids" that fill the front of her right leg, up to the top of her thigh, seem to take on a fiercely proud shadow of dark portent as she stretches her leg to admire them.

The scorpion on her shoulder, the symbol of the serial killer she locates, after she speaks to his victims' spirits, and who sends parts of his victims by mail, in a box, to their families. The nude nymph, with horns, smiles on her back, sipping from a marijuana leaf at the edge of the Oslo fjord, as her eyes glaze over from an opium rush. This nymph represents the beginnings of the opium deaths caused by addiction, during the years when fascism almost took over Oslo, until the people rebelled.

The other, smaller tats, the sleeping child angel, on her left buttock, the wide-awake, snarling child angel, on her right buttock, with his pitchfork, symbolize the loss of innocence that happens in a demon's heartbeat, within her beloved city, when the insane killer rampages on the island of camping children on 22 July, 2011and during the bombing at Regjeringskvartalet.

CHAPTER THREE: I LOVE YOU

What's that voice? Who's he in love with? Is it she? Another of her dream demons who regularly rapes her? "Mother?" she asks, wanting me to answer, but not expecting me to, which I rarely do, as my task is to watch her and not intervene in the land of suffering.

Why does she want to go out to see what or who it is? She pulls on her jeans, lying on the cot, and pulls on her turtleneck, woolen jacket, and red watch cap. She shoves her feet into the hiking boots on the front porch.

She thinks about the threat of war and the ogre Putin, the man she envisions as *la puta*, Spanish for whore. He's a whore to his own people, risking their lives again to gain political control over his rivals. Is this his computer voice saying, "I love you," a call to war from the Russians on Norway's one-hundred-twenty-five-kilometer border?

She can see this border just across the woods from her hidden cabin. It can all be a trick, and she might be gunned down, strafed as a Norse slut herself, because she works for the police in their perverted districts of male and female prostitutes. The Russian hackers try to take-over the Norwegian banks, government, and businesses every four seconds.

She has no weapon. The *Politiet* she works with don't have weapons available either. They're kept locked up inside the squad cars, only accessible when the lieutenants give the orders from headquarters. There's constant danger on these city streets.

But now she's in her own safe house. She often dreams she's a serial killer, and that she takes her demons inside to kill them through meditation and prayer to her Norse gods and spirits of Viking warriors—the Berserkers—who take apart their enemies with their bare hands, tearing open body cavities and eating hearts to shame them. She believes she has this same power inside, so she walks out into the forest to follow the voice of "I love you."

The odor of the birch, spruce, scots pine and alder fills her being as she strides into the woods in her snow gear. The streaked sunlight above the forest canopy looks like the Northern Lights have been dimmed by Odin, converting the primeval woodlands into a bedroom and playland for wood sprites, nymphs, and ogres. She listens for the voice.

"Jeg elsker deg!"

This time, it's a child's voice, not a man's speech. Is this another ruse by the Russians? Are they using their psychological warfare on her? Do they believe she'll become a coward like the former Ukrainian president was in Crimea? Her king, in World War Two, stood up to the Nazis, risking his own family's life to protect all of Norway. This is what made the Russian invaders friendly toward Norway. Has their compatibility, their shopping at Norway's businesses, their Russian citizens who live inside Norway, has all this comradery been forsaken forever in the heat of this new aggression by Vladimir Putin?

As the frosted snow crunches under her boots, and she shivers, she feels her nipples harden in the freezing weather. After hiking for half an hour, she spots her quarry. Ahead, she sees the source of the changing voice, a small girl in the clearing, encircled by six birches, which are gray guards hiding this tiny pale maid from Hell. Across the distance of about fifty meters, she hears her cry once more.

"Jeg elsker deg!"

Yes, it's the same voice, the girl she interviewed that morning, without coffee, without her morning meditation. She takes the binoculars out of her jacket pocket and looks. The demonic reality of this child has captured her poetic mind, as if Deadly Nightshade has been laced into her hot chocolate, which one of the officers brings to her out of pity.

How has this girl escaped from jail? Is she a spirit? No. Lily can see the flesh of her arms. Her entire slender body is bundled inside a red snowsuit. It's opaque crimson against the white birches' tree bark. Her long black hair blows restlessly in the wind.

My daughter inhales, and she swears she can smell the talc on the child's nine-year-old body, from where she stands next to the tall alder tree.

If the girl has escaped, then this is her unique chance to put an end to a future serial killer. Do society a favor. Lily knows that's what she will most likely become, a killer, and that no amount of counseling or therapy will rescue her from the hand of Satan. The State will soon forget, and Marilyn will be swept inside dens of iniquity, the slums and foster homes, the decrepit places where children like her are abused every day.

Most of all, this child is the spawn of a family like many of Lily's foster parents were. Bestial hypocrites who attend church on Sundays and molest their young on other days and nights at their weekly convenience. Then again, she reverses her thinking, the way she often does when she interviews psychotics. If she can *steal* this child and lock her away inside the safe house cabin, then maybe death won't be necessary after all.

Lily knows the Gnostic secrets and mysteries to train little Marilyn to fight against the lusting and greedy forces in the world around her. Lily survived, hadn't she? Lily hadn't killed another human being yet. Why can't she save this waif of the Devil, this little wolf, isolated from the pack, no matter how much the odds might be against her?

As in the Bible, Lily "girds her loins," by pulling up her jeans and shivering again, feeling the pink flesh on her face redden in the sub-zero weather, as she marches toward Marilyn, who's now standing, her short arms outstretched, as if she knows her female savior has arrived. The police and the state can't have her. Lily will train her, a sorcerer's apprentice, and make her into a strong woman who can prevail over all these terrible powers and become a psychic medium just like her teacher.

As Lily sprints toward the girl, the lighting above the tree line flashes, and the thunder explodes. She watches the flashing bolt hit the girl's body, and from within the smokey cloud walks a giant creature, a man, but a man who is bred beneath the snows, beneath the ground, and under all living things. This is a beast who can grab Little Riding Hood on her way to Grandma's house. To hell with the Big Bad Wolf! The Huldrekall drags his victims down into Hell itself, to be molested for an eternity, at his supreme pleasure.

The Huldrekall's eyes are sparkling, emerald-green, and his hairy, black torso is ripped, with mammoth forearms and muscular biceps. She feels her heartbeat begin to pound throughout her body, and when she sees the bulge beneath his loincloth, her passion is aroused. Is this really a fight to the death, or will she become a love slave to this dark-haired creature of the forest? The girl is obviously not there anymore. It's my daughter against a demonic force she has secretly worshiped in many of her dreams, written about in her poetry, and shown in her colorful art.

As she walks closer to him, however, she soon sees the reality. His mouth opens slowly, into a yawning cavern of black jelly that quivers under the midnight sun. The shark teeth are suddenly thrust from this quivering mass like razor blades hidden in *Exidia glandulosa,* or black witches' butter, which grows inside the dead branches of oaks.

The Huldrekall's tongue is pitch-black, and it creeps out of his mouth to slither, long and voraciously, against his hairy chest. The beast's wailing call to battle is so loud it shakes snow off the trees, the earth trembles, and she must cover her ears with her hands.

She remembers one of her foster father's sayings in Norwegian, *"Lily, du må alltid bekjempe ild med ild. Det er den eneste måten å beseire en demon!"* ("Lily, you must always fight fire with fire. It is the only way to defeat a demon!")

Lily's body begins to vibrate like an earthquake, and her thighs start to convulse, shiver, and pulse in tandem with the vibrant energy of the forever sun above. Her normal body now has a new form. She remembers Professor Seagraves telling her about there being no such thing as solid matter in the universe. Only forms and patterns.

She's becoming a pattern of the only true adversary to these male beasts of prey: Huldra.

As Lily runs, gliding across the snow as if it were a sheet of spun glass, she feels the power of her strong thighs, bulging calf muscles, and piston arms, rotating like Thor's hammers against her trim sides. She glances over her shoulders and sees the trademark spiny wood porcupine spurs jutting out of her naked back. The same doormat scraper she and the police joke about. She wishes they can see her now. She even hopes Putin can see her and understand the supernatural powers her native Norway holds in secret.

As she approaches the eight-feet-tall Huldrekall, she smells his anger and the slithering black tongue in his mouth sweeps across the front of his chest like the Marquis de Sade's whip inside his dark castle of seduction. She knows, as she enters the circle of his power, a drastic risk must be taken. This hazard is forbidden by all Norse supernatural law, but it must be done. Lily inhales, meditates as she holds her breath, and then she bursts forth with a ferociously trilling scream.

She stops. She watches, in awe, as the mammoth muscle monster stomps in the snow toward her. His breath clouds her face, and she sees her head being lopped off with one of his six-foot long arms. It goes rolling in blood, nose over ear, in the snow, but then she hears them, screaming, and running out of the woods surrounding the small circle of white birches.

Screaming like Irish banshees, the eight sisters attack him from all sides. Throwing kicks, flinging their backs directly into his huge torso, and biting viciously into his legs, arms, and neck. He's in trouble.

Lily smiles and watches, as the bloody confrontation continues. She will soon be escorting them back into their forest, as the big oaf is already on his knees begging for their mercy.

Roars from Hell itself erupt. The ground is cracking, and from beneath the surface of the snow mounds burst forth at least six Huldrekall monsters, and their faces are dark and brooding, eyebrows furrowed, green eyes flashing, as they concentrate on their prey. Fixing upon the women, Lily knows this is the end.

She sees dark clouds drifting from the mountains, and they're full of snow. Soon, it's going to be a blizzard, and she thinks this is a fitting way for them all to be killed. She isn't going to shapeshift back to human form. That's suicide. At least, with her spiny back, she can get a few good licks in as they fight to the end of their time on Earth.

Lily watches, transfixed, however, as the lead Huldrekall raises his long arm and snarls to his brethren, vapor clouds spouting forth from his mouth like a dragon. They halt their running attack and stand still, the snowy wind blowing flakes into their hairy chests like butterflies.

What's happening? Are these monsters from Hell toying with their lives? No. They are, in fact, smiling and pawing the snow with their giant feet in a stance of peace, submission, and romantic affection.

Just before the other women are romantically mounted, in the shadows of the nearby scots pines, Lily is able to transfigure into her human form, to the great consternation of her very large suitor. But he allows her to run off toward the cabin, and she smiles as she runs, at the prospect of mating with a Huldrekall, but she knows that in her dream that night she probably will mate with him.

Lily also knows that the next day, before she takes her poem to the printer's, she'll visit one of her spiny, love-soaked sisters, to find out how the loving was, and then give one of them the instruction. She knows that one of the Huldra's greatest feats is to be able to exchange a Huldra child for a human child, no matter the age, gender, race, or creed.

Astrid Lily Orkidedatter knows exactly for whom her sister, Olga, will be exchanging her child, as a Huldra can give birth in twenty-four hours. Lily will bring the girl to Olga and return with Olga's baby. She can change the birth dates, the identities, and Marilyn will be free, and one more Huldra will integrate into the Oslo population. What better teachers can there be to learn how to survive in the forest primeval, under the midnight sun, than her sister tutors?

Marilyn Southbine, the child who murders her abuser uncle, will be free to be wild, to kill, and to love, using the free survival will of the Huldra clans, including their spiritual leader, the Orchid's Daughter, who lives in the little cabin nearby. Marilyn will soon be eighteen, as her genetics will be changed and invigorated, the same way the Huldra conceives.

I am proud to be her mother, and I hope she can soon feel my pride.

CHAPTER FOUR: DR. SEAGRAVES

Before I begin, I first want to get our relationship straight. I am Dr. Martin Seagraves, fifty-seven years old, and I'm in fairly good shape for my age. I'm a lacto-ovo vegetarian, don't smoke, am an Advaita Vedanta philosopher, United States Navy veteran, who did two tours during our "forever wars," when they were taking anybody, even thirty-seven-year-old Naval Officer Reservists, and I'm also a recovered substance abuser, with twenty-six years sobriety under my belt (or in my brain, which would be a better cliché). Finally, I was also raped by six men, at age twelve, on a midnight fishing jetty in Seal Beach, California. This last detail was what gave me an immediate affinity with Lily Orkidedatter, age thirty-eight, of Oslo Norway.

Although I am first attracted to Lily's online sensuous poetry (I still have a working libido, and even the applicable "tools" still function), it is her deeper, more horrifically complex poems that make me want to know more about her and what she does for a living.

I taught college English for twenty-five years, as an adjunct, along with my work as a crime reporter, and Naval Reserve duties, so I want to show our artistic connection a bit more precisely, as it figures into our working relationship in this case. Lily's poem about Marilyn Southbine is the entire key to everything that happens.

Lily and I are bound together because we are both writers and artists (poets). Also, more specifically, we are sexual abuse survivors as children. Me, in the United States, she in her country,

Norway. I believe it is this connection, more than any other, that creates our psychological bond, and which leads to her permission allowing me to work with her on an increasingly complex case, which involves both rape (my experience) and incestuous abuse, coupled with a child's outrageous response, the murder of the adult involved, (Lily's experience).

Both Interpol and the Norwegian police in Oslo, she tells me, will play a major part in our case, and because of Lily's bond with me, and the nature of this case, which ultimately has international repercussions, I think it best to show our special relationship, most appropriately, through our poetry.

The poem Lily wrote, which is quite graphic in nature, deals with the initial child abuse case she works with, and it also demonstrates the intense psychological stress she endures on the job, which I want to capture for my readers who have little or no experience with cases like this.

It is my hope that Lily and I can reach these "non abused" readers by using our art, and our personal experiences. Even with our twenty-nine years of age difference, we both feel more comfortable working with children through their imaginations, rather than through the more lurid and mentally abusive techniques involved in police work.

As the police are run by the State, and the State is run by the Government, the levels of legal autocracy and bureaucracy can become quite daunting for we who are working the case from the trenches, so to speak, where the actual front-line toil with the abused and their abusers is much more like a dreamworld than it is any type of known legal or scientific world.

In other words, the level of abstraction at the higher levels has no relation to the poet's, victim's, or abuser's dream world abstraction of the experience. What do I mean by this? I mean that because Lily and I have direct experiences with the reality of rape, incest, and sexual manipulation, as well as the retaliation involved, we can communicate much better than any officer of the State can who has no such experience. This is certainly something police science doesn't have much patience with. But it is true for us.

I will try to capture Lily's world as she lives it, and my crime reporting experience will play a part in this case as it unfolds. As I said, her poem about the young murderer, Marilyn Southbine, has led to our bonding and discussing her case, and, as it so happens, it became our ticket to working together on this international sex trafficking ring and subsequent sting operation that can gain international attention.

As I said, Lily and I have the budget to work together on this case for fifteen months. She does have a little cabin outside the city of Oslo that she goes to whenever she wants to decompress from her psychological interviews. I have never been privy to its inner sanctum, but I can imagine what she does, as well as you can.

The demons she has of her own, she must purge through meditation (another discipline we share). Her poetry, and her visual art, have always given her this space she needs so desperately to recoup her mental agility.

I am mostly a loner. I never married, and my parents have died. When I'm not in front of other reporters, or interviewing detectives, Lily and I share a bond that is quite deep and affectionate. It can be seen as love, on many levels, according to guys like Erich Fromm and Carl Jung, and I miss her when she's inside her isolated cabin, "between the trees and the mountains," as she puts it.

Orkidedatter means "Orchid's Daughter." Like many women in Norway, she enjoys the symbolism of body art, and she also does visual art. It is the large tattoo of orchids she has on her right leg that I see as being a symbol of her personality.

In the "land of the midnight sun," an orchid is a delicate flower given on precious and romantic occasions. A new birth, a graduation, a wedding. As an orphan of the State, Lily needs that symbol to survive. She does it very well, and I hope my recreation of her work can begin to match her magnificent reality.

CHAPTER FIVE: MARCH 15

I do my homework about Oslo. It won the Green City Award in 2019, and as I am driven from the airport, I can see why. Trees decorate the inner city, as it has been a mild winter, in keeping with the global warming posturing of the big industrial countries, which Norway fights hard to deter. As the home of the Nobel Peace Prize, I am in love with the place already, even though Lily's dour comportment online often sets my teeth on edge about the place.

What I understand about Lily already is that her emotional baggage causes most of her depression and post-traumatic stress and not the magnificent scenery of her hometown. I know about this because of my own issues living in the paradise of San Diego, where I rarely take in any of the wonderful sights unless somebody is visiting from out of town.

It's difficult not to feel fresh and new in this community of environmentally conscientious folks. People jog, ride bicycles, and even skate on the sidewalks around Oslo. I haven't seen an overweight person yet since I got off my flight into Oslo Lufthavn.

I pay in advance for a year at The Thief Hotel, right in the middle of downtown. It seems somehow appropriate that I choose this place to call home. Tjuvholmen (Thief Islet), where the hotel is located, used to be a haven for smugglers, thieves, and scoundrels. Armed with the knowledge I now know about the city and its laws, I believe being in The Thief will help me balance my favoritism toward Oslo with a bit of dark history.

When I see Lily waiting for me, seated in one of the plush armchairs near the lobby fire, my face begins to exhibit the first joyous abandonment it has experienced in over four years. I run up to her and drop my luggage.

This woman has cast a spell upon me, and now I'll be working closer to her than I have worked with any human being, other than my fellow airmen aboard the aircraft carrier *USS Forrestal* in the Persian Gulf. After I witness how we obliterated downtown Baghdad, turning folks into flaming cockroaches with our superior air power, and then Iraq ends up having no weapons of mass destruction, I begin to have nightmares. When I receive my medical psychiatric discharge, I vow to never visit another foreign country again, until today. I am now in the home of the environmentally secure and peace-awarding city of Oslo.

As I hug her, I know I am home. Her face is radiant, and her Bette Davis eyes look me up and down, as my eyes also search her form. She wears a red-and-black lumberjack shirt and jeans outfit, complete with a red ski watch cap that hugs her blonde hair over her ears.

Her smile is like an elf's, rather demure and fragile, and yet when I hand her the poem I wrote during my flight, for this occasion, she lets out one of her "Viking warrior" whoops, as I call them, and snatches it from my hands, pulling me back down onto the couch so she can read it.

We've shared many poems and stories online, over the months, getting to know each other, and this is no exception to the way she behaves in virtual reality. She speaks superb English, with just a slight Norse accent, as she reads my poem out loud.

Several passing guests, and a couple of hotel employees even stop to listen to her. In a kind gesture that is quite a Lily trait, she translates the poem into her native language and reads it twice. I can't say my work is that good, but my face turns quite warm and flushed, even under my white beard.

OSLO POET (OH, SO SLOW)

As I read her, her soul, her ribald nature.
I must respond in kind for a moment.
The words must flow with passion,

As she makes me feel, Oh Slow, my darling.

She lives and breathes in the waves of snow.
The demons possess her body, in the season
Of undertow. The naked Viking woman.
Breathless, sucking in the sap of life.

Gorgeous in the new dawn, the purple shrouds
Heavenly mist of her whispers, white skin,
Erupting heart that never waits for him.
Dreams of his touch, his moments of towering joy.

Look out the window, my darling tattoo girl.
Orchid in the hands of the bride, of the swell
Of Jane Austin's imagination, watching him
As he crosses the fjord, smiling, ever smiling.
Distance never daunts her soul; she is Oh Slow girl.

Picking up colors, handling them with ease,
Stretching the light fantastically, with purpose.
I smell her colorful joy, in my heart of hearts.
Take a moment to listen to her dance.

She waits for him in the shadows. Surprises him.
His arms are open, his soul is as dark and playful
As her inner Poe sanctum of Elizabeth's bed.

Thank you, for this. My Oh Slow Viking.
Sanctum, sanctorum, blessed be blessed.
Dark and light converge at your breasts.
But they meet at your temples and inside
Your orchid's sweet crests.

Oh Slow Poet and Viking of the North
She loves even in her passionate dreams.
A dream of fierce victories, and bloody,
Fire-side demons at rest.

CHAPTER SIX: VALHALLA

March 2022, Oslo, Norway.

Although I am completely new to Oslo and its environs, I'm quite aware of its history, especially its most recent events. Lily took me to the tourist attractions, in her off hours, which weren't many.

Unlike California, Oslo has many open spaces filled with trees, parks, skating, and recreational sites, as only twenty percent of the land is developed. Certainly, the downtown is bustling, where The Thief Hotel is centered, but once she drives us in her Volvo past the business district, we only see open areas and nature, which is quite pleasant.

Oh. Here's my ditty about the place I now hang-out in during my months in Oslo with my new partner, Orkidedatter. Very cool hotel, by the way, so stay there if you can, even though my poem doesn't do it justice. I am in kind of a funky mood when I write it. The idea that there are real spirits and demons, is the farthest thing from my mind at the time.

THE THIEF HOTEL

I am here at the Thief Hotel. Oslo.
Where smugglers and pirates once held court.
My partner, Orkidedatter, is alive in the dark.

She shows me her heart, it is black at the roots.

I have never been anywhere else.
Only the Thief. Only the passionate loss.
Beginning life again after centuries.
After millions of lives of death and remorse.

Orkidedatter and I carouse downtown.
Calling to the health girls, massages.
Tattoo Parlor escorts.
Taking pickpockets for bus rides.
Dancing in the sewers of the mind.
Is the killer hunting again?
Did he steal the innocent?
Make cutlets from prime youth?
Salvage the millions of lost pussies?
Under the streetlamps of pubs.

I can't keep up with Orkidedatter.
Her dark thoughts move too fast.
The dark, the heartache, the blows from nowhere.
She was Cinderella, cleaning up blood
Inside her grandfather's Hulking den of pain.

I was alone, freaking out, looking old and tired.
Sitting in The Thief Hotel.
But the case is going to be international.
We need to move, Orkidedatter.
I can't keep up with your thoughts.
The moving snowplows stop my sanity.
I can't focus on any beauty anymore.

Where are your orchids of heaven?
The high black roses choking the garden's delights.
The killer's afoot in the red lights.
Orkidedatter and I are on the case.
Alone in The Thief Hotel.

The main street in Oslo, Karl Johan's Gate, has many pedestrian-friendly walkways and parks. Stretching from Oslo Central Station, near the waterfront, all the way up to the Royal Palace, this wide avenue passes many of Oslo's tourist attractions, including the palace, the National Theatre, the old university buildings, and Oslo Cathedral. I visited these in my first few days, while my partner was pursuing her case involving the girl who murdered her uncle.

I must say, Lily is very secretive about her side of the case, as she never tells me what her job entails, other than she is charged with doing "special psychological interviews and profiles" of police suspects. I do know she's technically called a "psychic and a medium," from our talks online, and that this plays an important role in her job, even with the police.

As I have already researched, Europe and Scandinavia, and especially Russia, are much more advanced in these practices of what our police would call "superstitious" areas of paranormal pursuits. Even hypnotism is frowned upon and wasn't permitted as evidence in U.S. courts.

Lily's job, however, is very popular with the authorities, and she is working fifteen-hour days on this one case. I know the police in the United States are also over-worked and underpaid, but the stress Lily experiences seems to be compounded by her emotional baggage from childhood terrors, which she somewhat compensates for by her art and poetry.

We are in a very good mood on the day she takes me to see Valhalla Castle, the new tourist attraction created on the former site of the July 22, 2011, attack, the island of Utøya in Tyrifjorden, Viken (then Buskerud).

The 2011 Norway assaults, referred to in Norway as "22 July," were two sequential domestic terrorist attacks by Anders Behring Breivik against the government, the civilian population, and a Workers' Youth League (AUF) summer camp, in which seventy-seven people were killed.

Earlier, eight more died and over two hundred were injured, in the bombing he committed with fertilizer explosives stuffed inside a van within Regjeringskvartalet, the executive government quarter of Norway. In my research, I discover that one in four Oslo residents knows somebody who has been harmed during this most grievous act of violence in Norway since World War Two.

Lily informs me that we'll be visiting a tourist attraction that's been created to help heal the soul of Oslo, with patriotic pride, and it has done just that. I am anxious to see this remarkable castle, built on the wreckage of such a monstrous event.

I wonder why we never build such monuments after all our "events" in the United States? We certainly got those Twin Towers Monuments up quickly. But nothing in Las Vegas for those victims, except perhaps for better shows and menu items for the "high rollers" in the casinos.

Or, what about the tiny tots, and tater tots at the hundreds of schools over the years with little gun control? No castles built there, except in the sky, perhaps.

We can see the castle on the road from the MS *Thorbjorn* landing, the same ferry that takes the AUF kids to summer camp. The structure is over eight stories tall, with Ninth to Eleventh Century Viking, or Norseman, decorations all over the outside of its surface.

Skulls, shields, head armor, broadswords, anchors, and chains, are fastened all over it. Online, it says it is structured by architects and craftsmen using the same the design as we saw in downtown Oslo at the Akershus Castle, which I'd seen earlier in the week. I read that the Akershus was built by King Hakon V in 1299 to ward off attacks from Norwegian nobleman Earl Alv Erlingsson of Sarpsborg.

"Whose idea was it to create such an attractive design?" I ask Lily, as we drive on the winding road leading into the parking lot in front of the castle.

She turns toward me, her thick brows furrowing in concentration. "Oh, I really don't know. Probably part of some big investment group that almost drove us into fascism. We have the same wage gap as you do in the States. Do you know that, Martin?"

I am pleased we are on a first named basis, not the formal distance we have online, but she seems a bit distracted, as I know this is the first time she's been on the island. She explains that she's afraid of the ghosts that are here, haunting the island, after the slaughter by Breivik. However, as I have been so insistent to see it, we are here.

"No. I suppose I get brainwashed by our Liberal media, especially in California." I open the door, catching my coat sleeve momentarily on the handle of the Volvo. "I'm not used to these cars, as I don't drive in San Diego. I take the buses and trolleys."

I quickly learn that when Lily walks, she doesn't dilly-dally. She is up the hill in forty seconds, and I find myself winded, puffing clouds of cold air, by the time I reach her at the portico entrance to the castle. She is straining her neck, staring up at the many windows in the gray structure rising above us, like a gigantic, grounded Viking ship.

On each of the eight floors of the building, which look like Akershus, a fortress, there are cannons in the portico windows, and I can see that it also has a central courtyard, where the tourists can congregate for photos during the summer.

The two church steeples can be seen on either end of the fortress buildings. Now the surface of the mostly brick façade is covered in hanging icicles and snow drifts inside the corners of the dark gray flat roof tiles at the top. We are the only tourists in this sub-freezing weather.

As I step onto the first of the fifteen brick stairs leading up to the entrance, I can see a bronze plaque on the side of the building. I punch in the Norwegian words into my cell phone's translator. It says:

"Thanks to the benevolence of Dr. Paul Balder, V, the father of Loki Balder, who died in the horrific shooting on July 22, 2011, we now have this edifice of culture, folklore, and tradition, dedicated to all free peoples, in all the lands that protect freedom, to the last drop of their blood."

I call to Lily, who is still gazing up at the façade. A squadron of rooks begins to circle the castle fortress, and their ruckus drowns my shout, so I call again, much louder, "Lily! Please come over here!"

She notices, half-smiles, and wanders over to where I stand. I believe her usual concentration has been affected by something, so I point to the plaque.

"So, do you know this fellow? Dr. Paul Balder? He seems to have been a big contributor to this impressive edifice."

Lily leans against me as she reads what the plaque says. Her alabaster fingers press against the letters as if she can feel what they mean on a deeper level than just words can express.

"Everyone knows this man. He is the biggest contributor to every event and special cause we have in Oslo. He owns most of the property of northern Oslo, and his business, Titan Energy, creates hydroelectric, solar, and windmill power plants for most of our downtown communities."

"What about his son? Was this why he built the castle? It sounds like a very tragic story."

She looks up at the building again and sighs deeply.

"Yes. In fact, he lives here, so he is close to Loki's spirit. In the Viking way, he is, in fact, considered a Shaman lord. A medium. I can feel his energies in this castle right now."

Lily places her hands against the side of the building, and as she does this, an old caretaker opens the swinging alder wood doors. He wears all black, with a turtleneck top, and his crow's feet encircle ice-blue eyes that squint down at us, as he shades his brow and bald wrinkled forehead from the glaring sun.

"*Ønsker dere en tur*?" He says.

Lily turns. "He wants to know if we wish to tour the castle."

"If he lives here, then won't we be bothering him?"

Lily frowns. "I must speak to you privately, Martin," she whispers. There's a panic in her face I have only seen once before. When she explains in an online call about her grandfather, Sebastian, who murdered two women on the farm he owned outside Oslo.

It had affected six-year-old Lily to such an extent that she began to flee out into the forest to escape what she told me was the "curse of that woman." Lily said her grandfather never buried her, so her spirit was haunting their house, even after her grandfather died.

"If you say so," I tell her, and we wave to the caretaker, and walk back down the hill toward our car. Lily sprints ahead of me, kicking up snow like a thoroughbred filly in the race of her life.

As I slide into the front seat, I see Lily's shoulders trembling, and she's sobbing, quickly clouding up the windows of the Volvo.

I place my hand on her right shoulder, and she finally turns toward me, as she wipes her red nose and swollen blue eyes with the back of her business suit's sleeve.

"What's wrong?" I'm worried she might be depressed.

"He knows! I saw the fox. It was hanging out of the window above the entrance."

"Fox? I don't understand. Who is he?"

She sniffles, and takes a deep, soul-wrenching breath.

"When I was a little girl, on the farm with my grandfather, he would get very drunk. He raged about my mother being a prostitute and told me I would be just like her. That's when I would go out into the forest to hide and commune with the spirits of our folklore that I read about in my books."

"I see. That sounds very healthy. What about the fox? Did you see one?"

"Yes! When the woman's haunting began, an orange and white vixen would come to visit me. She told me I could make this bad spirit stop if I said a magical chant. The words were in Norwegian, and I can't repeat them ever again, because then the bad woman's spirit could come back."

"Yes, and what happened?"

"It worked. At first. The woman's spirit didn't make things fly around my bedroom or cause lightning to strike our house during storms. But, one day, on the day my grandfather got drunk and killed the second woman, and buried her out in the field, he stood at my window. It was raining then. He held the vixen's neck, in his fist, and she was dead. The curses came back."

"And so?" I hold my breath.

"Somebody in the castle knows. I saw the same vixen's body hanging by the neck, at the end of a rope, outside the castle's window!"

CHAPTER SEVEN: THE FOX

Inside Balder Castle, as this is what he understands his home to be, Dr. Paul Balder, V, has contrived an especially devious architecture to provide for his secret delights. The woman, the freakish Norse spirit whore, Lily Orkidedatter, has now seen his first volley.

He smiles under his full, Viking walrus mustache and flexes his toned muscles as he pulls his jacket on in front the gold-framed, full-length castle mirror. The fox has been thrown out the window, like a gauntlet, and now she is aware of him.

As he struts out of the castle's main bed chamber, he holds his handsome head of blonde hair straight-and-rigid, as he is full of Viking Berserker spirit, as well as three lines of cocaine.

His rakish good looks, his Italian Sicilia-fit tuxedo suit with synthetic rhinestones, and with crimson-and-black cuffs and lapels, gives him, even at thirty-eight, the confidence he needs to appear before any media's hot camera, or at any social gathering around the world.

Photographs of all the victims of the bombings in Oslo, and on this now-sacred Utøya Island, are in 3D and hanging, like cathedral saints, on the stone walls, and inside his bathroom and den.

However, with the aid of Photoshop, he has replaced each head, of every victim, with the proud head of his only son, Loki. Loki, after all, is the authentic lord of this manor, and he speaks to him every day to learn what the true Demon King wants in the way of fornication, food, and frivolity.

His son always worships the teachings of the French poet, Isidore Lucien Ducasse, who once wrote under the *nom de plume* of Comte de Lautréamont. In his spirit form, in fact, Loki's image is the exact duplicate of this author.

His figure is thin, with curly raven hair and pasty white complexion, and he is nervous, forever moving about. His son's promiscuous inventions, however, take Ducasse's ideas from the great book *Les Chants de Maldoror* into an entirely new and sensually phenomenal dimension.

Dr. Balder's bedroom chambers are not part of the main tourist section of his castle. Instead, his private quarters are part and parcel of the ingenious plan he has devised for his clientele and for his staff of lovelies.

This kingdom of his is devised, under his direct supervision, into the architectural shape of Dante's Circles in Hell, with his playland serving as the heart in the circular mandala.

However, under his son Loki's direction, the different rooms are not the sins Dante used in his *Divine Comedy*. They are, instead, the more profane and realistic tortures and lusts included in Lautréamont's *Les Chants de Maldoror*.

Not one room in this scientifically ornate and beautiful monument to his version of worldly paradise, is connected in any way to the outside tourist sections of the castle, with their Viking memorabilia, patriotic art, tools, armor, and photographs of Norse leaders, kings, and queens. All these nationalist and fabricated images serve as the mask of phony democratic power.

Today, as all Dr. Balder's people know, his inner Circle of Maldoror is simply the frosting on his cotillion cake. His debutants are the most beautiful, the most treasured, the finest looking pre-and-post-pubescent nymphets—male, female, and every sexual identity in-between—money can buy.

They are presented to his secret clientele to provide all the profane and luxurious carnal and other enjoyment this world has to offer. It comes in the form of unbridled passion and creative play, in the most secure method ever created.

As most of his work is beyond this castle, Dr. Balder knows his face must be the handsome one. He is the living embodiment of environmental genius, philanthropy, protector of the downtrodden, and messenger of the future. He is full of hope and technological redemption of the species—human, animal, and plant—on this great Planet Earth.

Without this bogus facade, he knows, his secret rendezvous with the powerful can never take place. What he always knew, and what he decided to pursue once his family's name no longer was a problem, is that he needs the quest for international fame and fortune.

After his orchestration of the accidental death of his father, the industrialist Paul Balder the Fourth, the vainglorious attachments to the old Norway and its longing for free will, defense of democratic values, and constant call to protect the natural world, are seen by him for what they are: tribal masks. The powerful, inner circle knows the truth, but the masses must be placated.

What he sees as masks to hide profit for his family becomes the ingenious method to protect his famous clients and their secret hunger for Loki's passions according to *Maldoror*. What he knows from his industrialization of renewable energy, can work just as well for his secret and much more profitable venture of lust. If the rich and powerful are seen to be doing good deeds, on the surface, then their amusements, within each of the circles of diabolic pleasures, can be constructed right alongside the outside tourist amusements.

Dr. Balder often likens it to having an amusement park wherein, secretly hidden inside the frame of its outer innocence, are the sins of dark pleasures and palatial entertainment for the exclusive adults and titans of industry. If both his clientele and his well-paid laborers remain anonymously hidden, under their high technology masquerade, Dr. Balder can reap the profits of both worlds.

As he feels for the keys in his vest pocket, he smiles. Dr. Balder is very pleased with himself, as his adult amusement park inside the patriotic castle rise into his mind like the forms of the fifteen-year-old girls, who know they can hide behind their favorite music or a band member's identity.

His clients can enter a suite inside the Circle of Maldoror, a comfortable coven, especially designed for the girl to make love to him. The masquerade cloaks, or identity replacement technology, the latest DNA sequencing with CRSPR, from Russian scientists, can now alter looks for short periods of time They are the perfect shields for his middle-aged and older clients.

They especially enjoy the youngest ladies he can hire, and Dr. Balder understands the psychology behind his clients' yearning. The more wealth and luxuries one acquires, the more one wishes to savor the youth and vigor to keep these titans young. After the trysts, on the securely recorded videos he runs inside every suite, old men watch the girl's eyes follow every movement of their DNA deepfake identities.

His clients thrill even more, afterward, as if eating a Thanksgiving turkey sandwich after the main feast, when the girl's passionate and youthful body begins to gyrate and then squirm beneath their touch. Their robotic computer memories and brain chip implants give them the skills necessary to play the fan girl's favorite love songs, or Heavy Metal or Rap with their angry tirades.

Whether their old bodies are covered in the carefully sculpted identity of a newly clean-and-sober Justin Bieber, or a young Martinus Gunnarsen, from Norway, with his side-cut blonde hair and impish smile, it's always the passion of the girl's mouth, as it puckers, sweet and ready for that first kiss after the song, which makes the event worth every cent they pay Dr. Balder.

The money goes directly into his offshore bank account over the double-password and crypto-protected website. The Chinese and Russian hackers are his biggest threat technologically, but it's, of course the local witch, Orkidedatter, he has to dispose of first!

Dr. Balder carefully studies the others who have failed—Jeffrey Epstein and French playboy, Jean-Luc Brunel—who believe simple money and potential rewards of fame are enough to protect them from scrutiny. He takes secure steps to make his Maldoror Circles effective by using the masquerade of high technology.

Then, to double his safety, he makes certain to put his young employees into personal danger by teaching them how to invade the homes of the elderly and infirm, to steal jewelry and other valuables, and to be certain he had one of his camera crew with them as they committed the felonies. He thus has the blackmail evidence needed to keep these teens indebted to him and frightened of him.

He has also learned from his fellow industrialists who know to hire youth who are passionate about new technology and the designer drugs of music make-believe, such as ecstasy, THC, hashish, and even what the top executives of Silicon Valley enjoy, exotic tree frog venom, LSD, and ayahuasca plants.

To Dr. Balder, the world is open to opportunities, and his prospects have made him a billionaire, many times over, as the other billionaires struggle to make ends meet. Strike "when the fire is hot," is his motto. If your father is fading away and discussing giving all his legacy to charity, then kill him. Nothing can stand in the way of true progress.

There are no geniuses left, other than his profound genius, and this fact is what makes life a miraculous endeavor, every second. Dr. Balder's dedication to acquiring more prestige and power, as his only son, Loki, makes the true dedication to their spirit overlord, the poet Lautréamont. It metamorphoses into a game for the wealthy more profitable than any other match invented throughout world history. Better than the Romans and their Christian gladiators, the Americans and their cage boxing matches, or the Communists and their torturous gulags, the for-profit prisons, and all the other thousands of legal and profitable ventures.

Loki, and his genius application of Lautréamont's fantasies, combine with Dr. Balder's architecture of Dante's Circles of Hell, have made them millions of dollars in what began as a side-hustle in 2010. But then, it became a booming profit of hundreds of millions after the "Forever Wars" ended. And, when Putin finally invades Ukraine, in 2022, the money is unbelievably profitable. It's as if the more corrupt and powerful the leaders became, the more profit they make in their secret and sinful universe of passion.

In fact, Dr. Balder knows, simply by adding the cloak of personal identity secrecy, the same way their investments, like Private Equity Groups, give his fellow billionaires tax-free profits during COVID-19, as they invest in "homes" for the elderly, in which they cut costs, make profits, and kill the useless elderly and poor invalids, all at the same time.

To these world clients, it's an investment dream of Uncle Sam, Adolph Hitler, Vladimir Putin, and Xi Jinping, come true. If they can hide, he knows, all is well. This is the answer that far surpasses all the other would-be schemes of Bernie Madoff, Sackler's Opioid Family, and the Chinese and American Pharmaceutical profits. It's Dr. Paul Balder's dream to corner the market on this worldwide adventure in infamous greed.

As he moves into the next room of this Circle of Maldoror, he knows it's time to explore the next step in their plan to confront Lily

Orkidedatter. His son's spirit is in this palace room, and he keeps it dark most of the time, so he can commune with his demonic Mephistopheles, Comte de Lautréamont. Dr. Balder will light the torches on the stone wall, one by one, until he can see his son and begin their conversation.

Orkidedatter is the only person standing in the way of their final success. This international conquest will allow him to take over Norway and get rid of the farcical Royal Family and the pathetic history it represents.

This is the era of strong and powerful leaders who are connected to other strong and powerful leaders. One witch bastard whore is all he needs to defeat to become Norway's Prime Minister and destroy the Constitutional Monarchy forever.

CHAPTER EIGHT: RECONNAISSANCE

April 2022, Troldhaugen, Norway

Bergen, a stunning medieval seagoing city, perched on the edge of a fjord, is surrounded by steep mountains. Bergen is famous for its old wooden houses, narrow alleyways, open-air fish market on the wharf in the middle of town, funiculars, and cable cars creaking to the tops of mountains.

Lily has brought me here because she says she has something especially important to discuss about Dr. Paul Balder, his son, Loki, and Edvard Grieg and his home, Troldhaugen. How and why this last piece of information was added made me lose my fear of riding inside cars near plunging mountain cliffs (cars, to me, are none other than coffins on wheels) and so I go with her. I love classical music, and Grieg (like grief) is one of my favorite composers.

Being with my Lily in person, as opposed to the lackluster world of virtual, online "trolls," is quite exhilarating. I breathe in the fresh air, and I stick my white beard out of the window like a constipated, ancient Golden Retriever, until she finally pulls her Volvo into the parking lot of Grieg's home, surrounded by the fjord, the snowy mountains and valleys, and the woods where lurks these alleged magical trolls.

She has Edvard Grieg's "Peer Gynt" blasting on her CD player all the way from Oslo, and I am feeling right in the mood for her tale about magical trolls. Or else, I might want to devour a ton of Keebler Elf cookies.

Inside the Grieg Museum auditorium, I watch Lily listen to the piano man (they get a new one each week) play a more sedate selection of one of Grieg's pastorals, I feel I'm falling deeper in love with this woman than simply as a ghoulish romance of two people who experienced sexual abuse at the hands of real monsters. She leans forward in her movie theater chair, mesmerized by the music, as we sit with all the other tourists inside this little theater.

We are inside Grieg's house and the passionate atmosphere lends itself to thoughts of romance. Lily's blue eyes flash like Ukrainian, heat-seeking missiles, and I want to grab her shoulders, turn her around, and kiss her deeply, before she can tell me anything.

But I remain older, wiser, staid, and doctoral, waiting for her to tell me about what she needs to tell me. How is her psychotic girl killer related to this? What about Balder and his son? How does all this disparate information fit into her wondrously musical and mystical head?

The night before, we watch a movie in my hotel room at The Thief Hotel. We are both Ingmar Bergman fans, and the movie is his last, *Saraband*. I make a comment about how they show an eighty-eight-year-old composer's dick, but not the pussy of Liv Ullmann, Bergman's favorite Norwegian actress. "It's the opposite in the States," I say, munching on my popcorn. "Pussies galore, but hardly ever a dick is shown."

Lily stops watching and picks up her phone. She stares into space, and then, as if she were possessed by something out of this world, she begins to frantically finger-type on her virtual keyboard. I keep watching her in quick, sidelong glances.

When she finishes, she turns toward me, and she tells me a story about an online troll.

"Martin. There's been a woman trolling me. She reads my poems, and then she tells me she wants to be my friend. It soon became more than that. Now she says she wants to *be* me! I don't want to publish this poem because she will perhaps come after me again!"

I am concerned, so I say, "I understand. Let me read it. We can publish it another way that doesn't get onto your private website and blog."

As I read the dark poem, not unusual for Lily, I understand some of the deep tragedies coming to the surface of her mind. I am attracted and yet appalled, but I can't help but visualize myself as this poet's demon lover. It's crazy, I know, but seeing her beside me, after months of knowing her online, her fawning eyes and gorgeous tattoos now radiate toward me like beacons of supernatural passion. I can't help it. As I read, my heart swells with passionate urges to touch her, to cry with her, and to make her my own.

Rage Flogger in a Dungeon

I ponder that great mystery around your being, your shamanic flight of the rooted gloom.
You land upon my graveyard full of tear-filled orchids where Angels don't play.
Now and then when the night falls, this wondering has become my labyrinth.
A labyrinth of rainbow colors and shining drops of insanity but then, my demons attract me.

S T O P Listen, I can hear his footsteps, I can smell his scent.

I'm feeling weak, my body thrums like a witch drum, I take a deep breath, my mind knows what to do, but my heart tells me N O and my soul isn't listening. I want to immerse my whole self within his scent, within his skin, within his mind... I feel the weight of my eyes, and I slowly close them ... C L O S E. He is so close, I feel a touch of his warm breath upon my cheek, a tongue licking my jaws, and I gaze up into his ocean green eyes, so intense, so mesmerizing, and his hungry eyes are focused on me. Is this a dream, is this only my imagination, is this real? I hear a raspy voice shout at me; "I want you to say my name, the one you will be screaming soon..."

He lifts me up and throws me into a bed of bones. He puts on a skull over his face, then I realize these bones are from humans, and I know I have invited Hell into this battered country girl, into my safe cage and body... He roars, "You're mine!" I am marked for life inside my soul. He howls, "Release your inner creek and spill it over me." His dark mind is dangerous at this moment. I know no one can make love like him. No one can use lips like him. No one can caress my shapes like him. He awakens my inner starlight, my madness, my sins, and my nightmares.

I am lost in screams from this monster, a masterpiece, and a forgotten creature. We make love until the moonshine stops shining upon his beautiful face. I wake up naked, chained to a wall, shaking, and covered in cuts and bruises. I am playing with the fire, am I in deep trouble. Y E S I'm hanging from the wall, my saliva is drooling, I'm smiling, vicious, and I have his blood on my body. I am whole at last!

Back inside Grieg's musical auditorium, I wonder why Lily is putting off talking about why we came here. She seems distracted by something, and I don't know what it is. The fifteen-hour days she works on this case have perhaps taken most of her energy. She does look tired, with dark circles under her blue orbs, and yet as the pianist plays on, she seems to spark up, like a roman candle, to confront her demons inside. Finally, as the last chord is played on the grand piano, and we and the tourists applaud and stand up, I see a look of resignation on Lily's face, as if she's decided what she needs to do.

I follow her out of the auditorium and into the harsh light of the snow-lit day in Troldhaugen. She seems to know just where she needs to be, and I can see her pick up her usual speed of the obsessive-compulsive personality, and I must jump over lumps of snow and puddles of slushy-gray ice to keep her in my sight.

We seem to be headed toward the woods just beyond the thatched hut where Grieg did most of his famous compositions, including *In the Hall of the Mountain King*. This music, ironically perhaps, is now being broadcast over speakers in Troldhaugen as we step into the forest primeval.

I see Lily up ahead, her hands gripping the trunk of a giant alder tree, her white cheek against its bark, her eyes looking upward into the branches, as if they contain the answers to what she needs to hear. The music culminates in a thunderous cacophony, and she turns toward me, her eyes blazing once more with her mysterious energy.

I never know where she gets the renewed vigor, except that she tells me she is that "country girl" she references in her sublime poetry. Viking heritage, pagan spirit, and, to me, she is the Princess of the Dark Powers of Good.

She steps toward me in the shadow of the tree, as if she were approaching a fellow sprite, or gnome, which she has transformed by her secret powers. When I look deeply into her eyes, I can see who I am to her. I am in the shape of a giant troll. My head is huge, hairy, and has a bulbous nose that is snorting my cloudy breath into the mountain's frosty air.

My back is lumpy with twigs, crawling insects and worms as I bend toward her, my right ear, in the shape of a foot-long pear, points toward her, as I wait for her words. Was I becoming a part of the fantasy world she described to me in her work with the police? A world of Norse myth, the pathological lies of criminals, and her own horrendous experiences as a child.

When her words do come forth, I can feel the earth around the tree vibrate up into my boots, shiver my calves, penetrate my breastbone, and seep far into my brain until the words float inside my entire body, like a mesmerizing cloud of inky-black sounds, and tortured, animal yelps and screams. From out of this background comes her explanation of what she needs to do.

"Martin! Please listen, for I can only tell you once. As the world around us becomes more infested with evil, and tanks, guns, and missiles streak across the nightmare skies of trapped humanity, the girl I must send to Balder Castle is now living in the woods beyond my hidden cabin of refuge outside Oslo." She keeps one hand on the elder tree, as she speaks to me, and I imagine it's a direct connection to the distant forest about which she speaks.

"I don't understand," I say, and I expect my own voice to change into a macabre copy of hers, but it remains my human speech, perhaps a bit shaky, but still human. "Is this the girl who murdered her uncle? The same one you believe is connected to Dr. Balder in some way?"

"Yesssss!" Her voice sprays into the air, and, because of a COVID reflex, I bring my troll arm up to cover my face. "I saved her from prosecution, but the police don't know where she is. If I tell you that I can now send her and one of her Huldra protectors to the Balder Valhalla Castle, on the island of Utøya, would you believe me?"

My mind is crashing like a laptop, and all I can see is the pinpoint of light on my mental screen as it goes dim. I am a military man, a crime scene reporter. I have never heard such claims of spiritual powers as this. However, Lily's pleading eyes and voluptuous beauty of the night before in my hotel room, are still in front of me in the daylight of reality.

I reach out to her, take her two hands in mine, and I want to follow that with a kiss on those ruby lips, but I can't do it. I sense she is connected to another realm, far beyond my frail human ogre world. She should cast me bodily into that yawning forest, to be whipped by those Huldras, until I come to my insane senses. Was there a male of that species? I want to be anything other than the troll she sees me as now, who glowers inside her two beautiful irises.

"I have never seen anything, Lily. You know that. Your work in the cabin is secret. I can only take your word for what you can do. What evidence do you expect to find in such a spirit reconnaissance if it's even possible?"

"I must stop Dr. Balder from trafficking these people!"

"Stop him? Do you know the yearly amount of money made from world sex-trafficking is $150 billion? For the legal pornographic business, the figure is $57 billion. Let's see that's over $200 billion that's been traced, not including the amount that's never been discovered, including Dr. Balder's."

I feel her gloved hands shake from the cold.

"Dr. Balder has similar psychic and medium energies and believe me when I say he will send his own demons to confront any that I can conjure to send forth. I must first see what is inside his castle and what I need to do to prepare for what he is planning."

"What did you feel when you were at the castle yesterday?" I almost didn't want to hear what she might say, but my professor and journalist's mind was probing out into the Norwegian countryside. It was as if with every thought, I became filled with the same spirit magic my partner had within her.

"I felt how he's built a winding circle of lust inside that castle. This is what I must penetrate to see how we can plan our attack. Trust me. The child killer, Marilyn Southbine, has now been transformed by the Huldras into one of them. She has the Norwegian powers of their kind, and she is no longer a girl. She is now eighteen and a virgin of most sumptuous desire. When Dr. Balder sees her, he will be transfixed beyond his wildest and most lustful dreams."

"Dreams? Is this real now, or are you sending us into an inescapable Poe nightmare?"

Lily's breasts are heaving with passionate energy. "Let me do this, Martin! Dr. Balder will fall in love with her, and then she will be able to work her magic on him. Once she becomes part of his life, either as his mistress or his employee, we can discover what we need to know to combat his powers."

"All right!" I scream. "I am obviously powerless right now. Can you kindly change me back to my putrid old human form? Or do you have a thing for trolls?" As she tightens her grip on my claws, I can feel myself vibrate, and the possession of her spirit power seeps out of my frame, returning me to myself. I can hear the music begin again from the loudspeakers. Grieg's now familiar ode to the Mountain King pours across the forest valley, and I can see the earth break apart, revealing another creature in our midst.

He has a mammoth black head, furry ears, with a broad hairy chest and long piston-like arms. At about eight feet tall, his high-voltage green eyes pierce into me, as he begins to dance in the snowy sunlight, his matching black viper's tongue whipping the frosty air like a pendulum of death.

When he begins to move toward me in the shadows, I can see the teeth erupt from a black currant jelly inside the cavernous mouth, and I don't wait for Lily. I run as fast as my middle-aged legs can carry me, across the snow, into the parking lot, where her Volvo is parked. I stand beside it, blowing my heaving breath into the air, my eyes as big as flying saucers.

My partner, Astrid Lily Orkidedatter, smiles at me as she walks, slowly this time, up to the driver's side, unlocks the door, and climbs in. When I hear her unlock my side, I plunge inside, half-expecting the black ogre to grab me before I can lock my door.

CHAPTER NINE: MARILYN THE TEMPTRESS

May 2022, Oslo, Norway.

Now that I've become a working member of this paranormal adventure with Lily, I feel something beginning to change in my consciousness. Advaita Vedanta philosophers know that all so-called "reality" is constructed of sleep, consciousness, and bliss, and that we falsely assume that we are alone in an uncaring and destructive universe, when, in fact, the opposite is true.

The One in charge of this constant drama is the only unchanging and unknowable light force, and this so-called "reality" is what is always changing, and always will change, forever. It's that last part "forever" that tricks us most of the time. Why? Because of our frail little egos and our fear of death. That's why.

I know my psychic ability is basically null and void compared to Lily's. Whether it was the harsh cruelty she's had to live, or simply a gift from that One powerhouse behind everything, I'll never know. My sobriety and my wartime experiences have taught me a lesson about human frailty and humility.

I studied the teachings of a fellow recovered drunk and addict, and genius, John Bradshaw, and it was his concept of the "Wonder or Golden Child," which made me view folks in a much different way. He believed that we all have this inner child of wonder, and that it's society that destroys that wonder by its constant pressures to succeed, to compete, to be at war, and even to kill one another.

However, after you recover, and you clear your senses from your diseased mind, you can finally see this child inside, and that he can still exist and even grow. The Wonder Child then can overcome our self-consciousness, to allow us to be reborn into a kind of "spiritual outlook" that goes far beyond the selfishness of society's pressures.

To me, Lily is the Queen of the Dark Forces of Good, and I need to trust that this Dr. Paul Balder, V, is her opposing King of the Dark Forces of Evil. I know. This sounds too simplistic. Like some Marvel Comic plot dreamed-up by a delusional author. Well? Who isn't delusional these days?

I was raped at twelve by a wolf-pack of monsters on a fishing jetty, who didn't mind that I had nightmares for most of my life, not to mention my loss of male ego due to my father being a World War Two Pearl Harbor Survivor. I could never confess to him what happened, so I pushed it deep-down inside my consciousness, and I poured booze and drugs over that, hoping the rape would never bother me again.

Not so fast, grasshopper! When I heard a woman accuse a Supreme Court Justice nominee of sexually molesting her, and she said that she remembered "the laughter" most of all, my vision came back to me like a Poe nightmare, and I was able to confess it to gain constant sobriety. To understand me better, here's that story I wrote down and recited to my sponsor.

What does this have to do with our current battle against the unknown forces of evil in Balder Castle? Let's just say that my story will give you a mental image of Dr. Martin Seagraves, before he became the Iraq War veteran Seagraves, and the college professor Seagraves, and the Crime Journalist Seagraves. This is my inner, wonder child, Seagraves, who today believes in the powers of my partner, Lily Orkidedatter, a wonder child beyond my wildest dreams:

Back to the laughter. Martin is on time. The sun is disappearing beneath the western horizon. Blood red and frighteningly huge, the revolting anger building inside Martin seems to join this ball of fire, as it plunges down below Earth's painful reality. He now feels nothing inside except a longing for adventure. He wants an experience that will place him on par with his father, the Pearl Harbor Survivor, who jokes he is really a "Grand Pearl

Farm Survivor" because he came from a family of fifteen, and the judge at his trial, in 1940, for "drunk and disorderly" tells him he can either join the military or go to jail.

It happens almost immediately.

"Hey, kid! You gonna do some night fishin' too?"

Martin can smell something strange. The cigarettes in the hands of these older boys smolder. Unlike his father's long, Pall Mall reds, which create circles and dance in the waves of light, this smoke is languid, and the cigarettes are short and stubby, pinched between the thumb and forefingers of these hands like dog poop.

As he glances from one of these older boys' heads to another, Martin sees the same wincing, strained expression. Deeply inhaling the magic smoke, each one has a pained expression, as if a screaming demon perches on their shoulder, teeth poised to sink into flesh, and these boys know they must act quickly to save themselves from being devoured.

This can be the adventure Martin so longs to experience! He has already devoured *Treasure Island*, and was transformed into Jim, watching Long John Silver trick the stupid authorities and take him to the place where the real wealth was contained: the descriptive and sensory reality of hunting for treasure. Then, there was the world of Tom and Becky, inside the dark cave wherein Injun Joe lurked, a shadowy figure of fear, until Martin's mother told him his own great-great-grandmother was an Indian from Canada, "a Mi'kmaq," were her words.

When Martin saw his own father fight the dark man who stepped out of the car, which contained his mother, he wanted so much to see his father win. When this dark man slammed his father down to the alley dirt, with his fists, until he was bleeding and beaten, Martin's mind saw the man as one of the Indians his mother had recruited from her side of the family. Injun Joe had pummeled his father and caused such a loss. When he later called his mother to ask her to return to his drunken father and him, Martin had flashed the image of Injun Joe in his mind, and this villain was holding his mother captive inside his cave. "No, Martin. My love, I can't come back. Your daddy is cheating on me."

When she never appeared in court to give her side of the divorce argument, Martin was certain she had been taken into the tribe of Injun Joe and would never return. In effect, she never did, to his childish mind. Except for one brief telephone explanation when Martin was eleven.

"Why didn't you want me?" Martin had asked her, wanting to know why she had never wanted to have him visit during those years apart.

"Dan said he would break my nose. He didn't want kids."

Martin understood. This Injun Joe was a violent man, and this was also a violent world.

"You wanna hit, kid?" The tallest of the older boys is talking to Martin. His arm is stretched toward the young boy, with the smoking, yet possibly magical cigarette thrust at him, and he then pulls it back, in a see-sawing motion of beckoning. To his young mind, what they wear is uninteresting. The details are not implanted in his hippocampus. It is growing dark all around, and they may as well be pirates gathering around a campfire on Treasure Island, counting their loot from that day's marauding on the high seas.

"Are you guys pirates?" Martin asks.

My thirty-seven-year-old-self cringes when I hear him ask that. Was I that mentally stupid at twelve? Did I crave adventure so much that I would transform these obviously sinister older boys into fictional characters? As I later learn, after reading such monumental and psychologically profound novels as *Catcher in the Rye*, *The Lovely Bones*, *Deliverance*, and *Prince of Tides*, what my younger self is experiencing that moment is a profound shift in perspective.

The event I am about to experience is easily suppressed into what I now know to be my "deep sleep self." However, my adult audience, any decent Upanishad scholar, will tell you that even in deep sleep existence, the seed of Maya dwells, as it is the grand illusion we mistake for reality.

"Hell yeah! We're some real pirates. Come on over. We got some sweet grass, and we even got beers. Right, pirates?" The tallest boy opens his arms wide, as if by so doing he can change these darting and mischievous heads and eyes into a single pirate identity.

Martin has smoked before. On Grand Pearl's farm, he stuffed cow hay into his Grand Pat's rolling papers and smoked them. He and two Catholic school pals smoked his father's Pall Mall reds on the way home from school. Martin's job as altar boy did not preclude such experiments. When he inhales the smoke from this cigarette, however, he instinctively knows it will be different. And it is.

Before I get into what you've been waiting for: the gang rape of a twelve-year-old by six would-be pirates, let me first discuss political correctness on the part of some Liberals. As a former college professor, and writer for over twenty-five years, I believe I have the right to link it to my story.

Homosexuality, these days, has become almost a sacrosanct topic in the major media and in the halls of academe. Strictly speaking, the "actions" of homosexuals should always be open to criticism, and I am certain my gay friends would attest to this. There are those homosexuals, for example, who argue vehemently that they should have the legal right to rape underage boys.

They, of course, substitute the diametrically opposed word "rape" that I used, for the more acceptable, to them, word "love." To them, if the child agrees to participate, the act will be one of loving and physical devotion to that child's blossoming into a sexually aware adult.

To others, including this observer, because a child is supposedly proven to be protected from harm by others—either psychological or physical harm—until he or she is of the age of eighteen, the issue of consent is moot. A child under eighteen cannot consent because he or she is not an adult. End of legal argument.

Emotionally? Insert paradox here. I also believe in "old souls." These are so-called biological children who have the intelligence far beyond most adults, and this is not merely intellectual intelligence, it is also emotional intelligence. Are these geniuses, therefore, adults in nature? No, I say, because these child prodigies merely mimic the adult world, but theirs is the same magical thinking realm that little Martin is now facing. Children are smaller, more fragile beings, equipped only with magic to defend themselves. They should never, under any circumstances, be forced to endanger that beautiful and innocent fragility.

After Martin inhales the smoke exactly the way the older boys teach him to do, keeping it in the lungs for a count of ten, he begins to understand what being magical can really mean. He takes in at least four more such inhales, and drinks two of their many cans of beer, which now litter the rocks around the fire pit like the armor of fallen warriors ("Yeah, kid! That's what they are! Dead soldiers!").

"Let's take off our shirts, men!" The tallest pirate says, pulling off his tee to expose a very muscular torso. The other five do the same thing, although these boys are of lesser muscle development. One is even quite fat, with folds of flesh bouncing at his midriff like a deflated innertube. "Hey, tie your shirt around your head. That's cool. Like real pirates."

Martin smiles at them. He is enjoying this play-acting, as it is his lifeblood. When he is eight, after having seen the movie of *Peter Pan*, Martin convinces the other kids that they can fly. Even Fatty Patty jumps off the roof of their playhouse because Martin tells her to do so.

Unlike today, when video games and movies have transformed reality into a much more real experience, Martin and his generation had to use their imaginations to create the reality around them. During that night on the jetty, Martin knows he is staying out after his curfew, and even though his father is on one of his escapades searching out hidden communists, or "drinking and whoring," Martin is still in danger of discipline by adult figures.

This new experience, however, is too good to pass up. "Sure, I can play too!" he tells them, and he whips off his shirt, even though he's hairless and shivering, his skinny chest dimples with goosebumps in the salty, yet warm summer air. He, also, ties his tee around his head. They all look like suburban pirates, dancing and whooping around a blazing fire, telling tall tales of adventure in the glowing darkness.

"Hey, kid. You know what we do to be real pirates? We play our game called circle jerk. The first one who comes is a jerk!" To Martin's shock, and still to this day, to this older man's shock, each of the older boys unzips his jeans and pulls out his penis. Martin knows what his penis is, and he even knows what procreation entails, having been instructed at age eight, by his father, in the back of one of the taverns he frequented. His father had Martin recite the "facts of life" to his girlfriend from inside the tavern.

Martin's penis, however, is very small compared to these boys, and it has very small puffs of pubic hair around its shaft. Quite embarrassing. He can get hard, but he has yet to experience an orgasm. These other pirates, however, are jangling their penises like rubber chickens, and these chickens, like the ones Grand Pearl drew from the bubbling water cauldron, are loose and limp, hanging down with embarrassment, it seems, in the fire's glowering brightness.

That's when the laughter begins. The hippocampus memory that triggers him from deep sleep by Dr. X and her Internet testimony. These five older boys are laughing. And then, most horrific of all to Martin, they begin to sing a song.

"Roly-poly, dick-in-my-holey, look at the slimy goo! Rub your nuts, across my guts, and join the horny crew!"

Laughter, hooting, and unrestrained lust combine with an inner force that is unmistakable, even to a twelve-year-old boy. When the tallest, older boy pushes Martin face-down on the patch of sand next to the fire, the adult piracy begins, and the childish imaginary pirates end.

First, his jeans are yanked off his hips and over his feet. Martin is looking backward, craning his neck to see what's happening. He thinks they're doing this because it's the only way he can become a pirate. "Do I have to, Long John?" Martin whines, as the older boy grabs him by the curly brown hair, and yanks his head back, like a bucking bronco. Martin even snorts, at one point. But, when the big boy inserts his hard penis into Martin's bottom, the fantasy takes on an even more macabre reality. He's lying on the bed, waiting for his drunk father to administer punishment with his belt. "Ten welts for that mouth of yours! No backtalk! Get your hands away! Take it like a man!"

Pirates must be dirty, and this is the dirtiest. It's so dirty; it can't be written about in the adventure books Martin is reading. They aren't even curses written on Injun Joe's cave wall. Certainly, thirty-seven-year-old Martin could understand the reality of being raped—even in literary terms—but to child Martin, it has all become an horrific, secret ritual that can never be shared with another human being, lest the magic of its act be lost forever.

One by one, each of the older boys takes his turn. Martin's mouth fills with sand, as he digs his face into it, like an ostrich, trying to escape. The pain of being entered from behind is growing above his protective imagination's world and into a Hell of itself. They are no longer pirates. They are snorting, yelping dogs, pumping on the front lawns of America. Moms must bring out the hoses and spray them full force, because they're hung-up, refusing to come apart from this vicious, most animalistic love.

However, it's the laughter that makes them human. They're enjoying their lust, despite Martin's cries of pain, and despite his shouts of hatred. "Get off me! You fucking morons! You degenerate scoundrels!" They laugh at his words, and they laugh even louder at his use of big words. "Kid's gonna be a pussy when he grows up. Fucking bitch!" They shout down at him, spitting on him, waving their flesh wands, pornographic Merlin wizards, as his groggy, inebriated mind darts images inside his skull like a manic, old-time movie. He's Charlie Chaplin, the Tramp, getting buggered in front of his girlfriend. He's, most horrifically, Jim, being had by Long John Silver and his entire crew!

When Martin feels the blood begin to flow out of his mouth and through his nose, after being struck in the head so many times, he begins to enter deep sleep. And, when the blood begins flowing between his butt cheeks, from the penises that have pounded him down there, forcing him deeper into his dark sleep, all he can remember are the catcalls, the jeers, the curses, and the refrain of that ever recurring, and abhorrent song.

So, now you know. This is the story I showed Lily the first time we met online. It was what bonded us like no other existential incident. She told me about her life. The intelligent prostitute mother who at first had given Lily to her grandfather, and she was a six-year-old who witnessed his murder of two prostitutes on the farm. This led to Lily watching the dead fox vixen he held outside her bedroom window that fateful day. Of course, when the police discovered her grandfather's infamy, they put the child Lily into the circle of abuse called the "Oslo Foster Care System."

This all took place during the attempted fascist take-over of Norway, so when Lily was abused, sexually violated, and tortured by her captors, over the years of her childhood and into adolescence, nobody was there to help her. Her mother, Ingrid, the prostitute, died in downtown Oslo at the hands of a john who thought he was a werewolf and was later "rehabilitated" by the same system that controlled Lily's life. Today, Ingrid's ghost, when she goes to the Oslo gymnasium where he works, sees him teaching children. She is aware, without his medication, that he can become a monster, and perhaps one day he will kill again.

Now, as I think of another child that Lily has rehabilitated, in her own way, with these mythical Huldras from the forests behind her cabin, I don't cringe. I know Lily's magic, and I have faith in her. This child, Marilyn, she tells me, is eighteen, a virgin, and she no longer wants to kill adults, unless they are evil incarnate, which is what Lily tells me this Dr. Paul Balder is. I believe her. I have faith in her. There are demons amongst us, and unless we can get rid of them, our society will one day be forced to pay the price of harboring such monsters in our domain.

CHAPTER TEN: BALDERDASH

No matter how busy his schedule, Dr. Balder always makes a daily appointment to converse with his son, Loki, inside the private castle room next-door to his own boudoir. The entire philosophy of his business with these world billionaires and political leaders depends upon how creative Loki is with his sensual content.

His Titan Energy Company represents some of the wealthiest people in the world, with whom he socializes on a regular basis. Once he's able to get them alone, to probe their individual psyches, and their unique tastes for exotically produced pleasures of the flesh, it's his closing contract that wins them over.

Like a business contract, they simply want to be assured their private interests are protected from public scrutiny at all costs. The ones who have no such carnal tastes, of course, are passed over, but they're in the minority, thus far.

The pressures of their lives, their business dealings, their home pressures, and simply the realization they're at the top of the heap in the world's competition, usually make Dr. Balder's proposition very acceptable. The fact he can promise them complete anonymity, and a disguise that hides them from plain sight, makes his son's smorgasbord of sinful pleasures that much more important to his bottom line. Therefore, he's not about to allow one local Oslo woman, who's obviously mentally deranged, to get in the way of his perfected inner sanctum of pleasures in Valhalla Castle and around the world.

It's the problem of Astrid Lily Orkidedatter that he wants to discuss with his son's spirit today, as he enters the darkened room. Dr. Balder always sits in the same place in the darkness, just to the left of the grand piano, where he has it mechanically playing Edvard Grieg, the patriotic musical father of Norway, as they discuss business strategies together. In fact, he often whistles "In the Hall of the Mountain King," which he believes is his theme song.

He has already done a thorough background search on this woman, and once she appears, he's ready to accomplish his goal of putting her in her grave before she can do any more damage. When she ran from the castle, that day, he knew it was time to begin the process to end the lives of this witch and medium along with her guest from the decadent West, Dr. Martin Seagraves.

The voice of Loki comes at him in the dark, and he can see the face of poet Isidore Lucien Ducasse, pale, smiling, and sinister, hovering in the air like a demonic Cheshire Cat. This is always Loki's preferred mask, as *Les Chants de Maldoror* are his biblical stories.

Father, you should not kill the bitch so fast. She is more than a witch, you know. We already have our spies out to keep watch. We can use her to test more sensual activities for our clientele around the world.

This is something new. What can he mean? "I thought we needed to have the supernatural realm free from this woman. She seems to have the same powers we have. I don't know of any other person who embodies these powers of the dark forces."

I understand. But she is something else. My master tells me if we can capture her rare essence, by seducing her, we will achieve supreme dominance over her. Listen to the plan, father. We will use this sexually obsessed and violence adoring woman to test out the newest phase in our Maldoror Circles. It's a plan that will make us the wealthiest company on Earth!

Dr. Balder's breath becomes faster, and an erection begins in his pants, swelling his member to a plump and ripe cucumber. "W ... what is this plan, son?"

The glowing spirit of Loki begins its pacing, back and forth, turning toward him only to glare and smirk in the darkness of the room. The piano swells to a fever pitch with its Mountain King rhythmic beat.

This bitch's mother, Ingrid, is under my power! I sent her as a spy. She says her daughter fantasizes nightly about making love to Norse creatures, demons, and other dwellers of the night. I have contacted this whore mother, and she is going to place a curse on her witch daughter. She wants to meet the Huldras, who live in the forest behind her secret cabin in the woods outside Oslo. She wants to know from them what it was like to fuck a Haldrekall. This is our chance, can't you see? You will appear in your white Huldrekall disguise, to find out how much enjoyment this can be. Your rule in the spirit world must be proven more powerful than hers before we can conquer the world.

Once again, his son's genius astounds him. In fact, he has his entire castle equipped with hidden cameras, twenty-four hours a day, so Loki can enjoy the fantasies of his clients. Now he learns this woman has similar fantasies as he? What could be more perfect?

"Yes! I will do it, my son. I knew your death was never in vain. What else do you have planned? I know you are never without other cards up your sleeves."

Quite right! We must also find out what has given her this power. Her whore mother doesn't know, or she refused to tell me. If you can fuck it out of her, so much the better. Is tomorrow a good day for you to tryst with her? Take her to the waterfall, father. Women always swoon when they can feel the urgent release of nature's passionate force.

"Yes! I must meet with two new employees who are going to help me promote the new masturbation law, but then I will be free to go there. I think this is an astounding plan, my son!"

Dr. Balder can feel the exact GPS location being transmitted telepathically from Loki's spirit consciousness, and he files it away into his photographic memory.

Don't allow her to gain the upper hand, father. Our entire plan can go awry if we don't learn where she got her powers, so we can use them against her once the time comes.

Dr. Balder stands, shuts off the piano, and walks toward the castle door. He turns and watches his son pace and moan with expectant passion. The only sexual release, he knows, comes when he, his father, has sexual release. Perhaps he'll try to have some fun with the two Russian girls, Marina and Olga, before he transforms into the Huldrekall at Lily Orkidedatter's forest retreat.

The world is so much more enjoyable when Dr. Freud's Libido can be released and becomes satisfied to its fullest extent. The sexual fantasies of his dreams are filled with violence, control, and energy beyond human comprehension. This Lily plaything will enjoy the full measure of his lust and perfected sexual prowess.

"*Abiento*, Loki, my son! Enjoy me tomorrow. I will make you proud once more. I will learn all I can for you."

CHAPTER ELEVEN: INGRID THE CHAPERONE

My daughter, Astrid Orkidedatter, who likes her nickname, "Lily," probably because I don't, has given me this assignment. I am to chaperone the living embodiment of the "formerly" psychotic child, Marilyn Southbine, who, according to Lily, has been grown with genetic transformation by Huldra blood, and rehabilitated by the clan of forest dwelling Huldras into one of them. In fact, as I can see, there's another one of these young ladies accompanying Miss Southbine, and they are both eighteen and quite fetching, on their journey to Valhalla Castle on the island of Utøya in Tyrifjorden, of Viken.

As I cannot communicate with these two ladies because I am considered a "restricted ghost," which means I am mentally attached to only one person (my daughter), upon whom my eventual release from this wheel of constant sorrow depends.

These two young ladies, who are now approaching the ferryboat that will take them to the island, are riding a Vespa motorcycle, their dark hair blowing freely in the freezing and clear, Norwegian air. I, on the other hand, am floating easily above them, gazing down, and recording their activities.

My daughter likens me to a drone electronic device, which were not invented when I had a body, but after she described their ability to do everything, from spying like a Peeping Tom, to bombing alleged terrorists, I quickly became enamored of this duty.

With her obvious supernatural talents, my mental recordings will be transmitted telepathically back to my daughter, so she and her erstwhile partner and resident strange person, Dr. Martin Seagraves, can plan for their eventual attack on the castle where our villains reside.

It's quite thrilling, and I look forward to my job, as the more I can show I am worthy to the unseen powers in control of my future, the more I can feel at peace. Being stabbed by a mental case werewolf was not a good way to pass, you can take my word! Combined with an ungrateful daughter, a mother's duties, it would seem, never end.

My daughter did explain how she had procured employment credentials for the two women below me, who are now pushing the bike onto the ferry, ready to cast-off and make its way across the fjord to the island. It seems Dr. Paul Balder hires many Russian women for his duties inside the castle, as he works closely with the Russian scientists for other purposes, about which the Oslo police have no information.

Therefore, Marina Alexeev (Marilyn Southbine) and Olga Sarkov (identity given to the Huldra), are two Russians who live in Oslo, close to the Russian border, near Lily's cabin in the woods. They have an appointment at 0900 to interview with Jorunn Olsen, the Human Resources Officer at Valhalla Castle.

If hired, Marina and Olga will proceed to do their sleuthing, and Marina will make her attempt at seducing Dr. Balder to gain access to the inner chambers of the castle where he conducts his secret business operations with unknown clients. Although the police know that many private jets land at the Oslo airports, once they take up residence at hotels downtown, they are never seen again until a few days later, when they are whisked back to the airport where they first landed.

Whether or not these important people visited the castle is not known. My daughter said she believes this is one of the main secrets Marina/Marilyn must discover. The other information to uncover is for me to see what kinds of spirit demons might be occupying this castle of his.

From my experience, both as a prostitute on the streets of Oslo, and as a spirit haunting my daughter, it's not the spirit dominion, I fear. It's this so-called "real world" right down there. I must now drift on down to be next to these two girls as they interview with Dr. Balder's representative.

This should be good! He is the same fellow who tried to clean-up the immoral sex trade in Oslo for his fundamentalist religion voting base. He wants to "protect Norway from sex!" Good luck with that, I say!

"Well, Marina and Olga. It looks like your references are in order. You both have the experience Dr. Balder needs. I must ask, however, do you mind being monitored for our top security purposes? We will not violate any of your personal privacy, but we must keep our inner sanctum secure inside Valhalla Castle."

This woman looks like Boris Karloff's sister. Lily enjoys the late horror movies inside her cabin, and I must watch them with her. Dressed in all-black, this woman has her German bun hair and giant wire-rimmed glasses. She leans forward as if she might devour our two lovelies and chew them raw for lunch.

Lily's little reformed psycho also leans forward. Her purple lipstick contrasts well with her rook-shiny hair and pouting expression. The perfect nymphet Lolita for Professor Humbert-Humbert.

"We don't mind. We are from Russia. Mr. Putin likes to monitor citizens also. But, please, Miss Olsen. Will we ever see Dr. Balder? He is why we have applied to your organization. He is such a patriot and genius for our environmental causes! I pray for him every night. Many powerful people want him dead. That's what they say on social media."

The straight woman sits up straighter if that's possible. She brings out a piece of paper. It looks like a memo of some kind, with Dr. Balder's picture on the letterhead.

"It's very interesting you say that, Miss Alexeev. Do you mind if I call you Marina? As you must know, we are all quite frightened in Oslo about the recent unrest in Ukraine. All of Europe seems to be quaking right now from your country flexing its muscles."

Marilyn (Marina) nods. "Yes, call me Marina. I understand. That is why we moved to the Norway side to live." She laughs. "But Europe has also been moving its nuclear weapons closer to Russia, and it is like a big game of chess, no? Black versus white. The king must always be protected, at any costs. My king is Dr. Balder, as he is a progressive man."

"Yes. Dr. Balder has just supported a new law that was passed yesterday by the Parliament of Norway. He wrote most of the rationale for this law, as he believes it will clean the streets of our worst scourge. Pedophiles and perverts. No God-fearing nation needs to see this happening in their midst!"

The Huldra, Olga Sarkov, speaks up. "The Huldrekall menace? Is this what he means?"

The middle-aged woman squints at Ogla. "Huldrekall menace? Isn't that Norse mythology? We may need to give you another test, Miss Sarkov. Do you believe in such creatures?"

Marilyn kicks her partner under the table.

"Oh, no! I just meant this to be a metaphor for any of the underworld gangsters we have in our recent crime wave," Olga says.

"I see. Very well. No, this legislation will put a stop to the flagrant exhibitionists and pornographers in our midst. It is worded in such a way as to trap any acts of sex—homoerotic or heterosexual—that happen in public. This includes masturbation by individuals and acts that can serve as masturbation fodder for the perverts who might film it on their phones and cameras."

"Oh my! That is innovative. But what if lovers are simply in nature, and they want to show their love for each other?" Marilyn is smart to ask.

"Dr. Balder believes those acts must be private. In fact, there is a clause that can convict anybody who doesn't close their windows. If an official sees such perversions being exhibited within the domiciles, then they can be charged as well." Mrs. Olsen smirks. "But his true genius is that these guilty people will not waste taxpayers' money by being housed in our jails. No. As Dr. Balder is a big fan of literature, he is always enthused by the American author, Nathaniel Hawthorne's novella, *The Scarlet Letter*. Dr. Balder's new holographic device, he calls the 'M Machine,' will create a large letter on the back of each person convicted of violating this act of indecency, and they will be registered as public sex offenders as well!"

Marilyn smiles a crooked grin. Her psychotic mind seems to be working now. "That is genius. Remember that film in Germany, in the 1930s? Fritz Lang's *M*, about the child molester, who is caught by the people, and marked with that letter so they can catch him? So, this letter 'M' will show on the backs of these deviants?"

"Oh, yes! You are well versed in your classical film knowledge. Dr. Baldwin will like that. That is exactly the way he proposed to market it to the Norwegian public. How insightful you are!"

"Thanks, Miss Olsen. So, where do we fit in here?" Marilyn asks, running her alabaster fingers through her long black hair.

"As I said, this legislation is being marketed to the public right now. We need models to portray innocent damsels being victimized by these perverts. Of course, there will be no shots of the monsters, themselves, simply reaction shots of our ladies and gentlemen. Can you portray looks of horror or aberration effectively?"

Old monster pantyhose leans forward again, a gleam in her eyes that imagines the two girls naked, one supposes.

Marilyn looks at her partner and foster mother Huldra and smiles. When she turns back to Olsen, there's a gleam in her eyes. With Marilyn's history, one imagines she's sizing her up to be cut into nicely shaped flesh pieces to insert into her toys.

"We'd love to be part of this effort! Lead the way, Miss Olsen."

CHAPTER TWELVE: LILY'S FIRST LOVE TRYST

I must convince my daughter, for her own good, to meet with him. She has always been a rational girl, except during her work with these violent psychotics, serial killers, and other perverted souls. She becomes so impassioned and depressed, at times, I can't stand it! I watch her nightmares, and they flare into my own being, until I must awaken her.

I know if she can serve a purpose by living out her passion, the way my father did on his farm, then she will be free to work in peace at last. And, with the good Dr. Balder supporting me, I will be released from this purgatory of spiritual imprisonment.

What's she doing now? I see. She's authoring another of her strange poems to release the demons of her mind. I will look over her shoulder to read the flow of her mental aberration. She's like an insane Henry James or Proust, perhaps even Virginia Woolf. What do they call it? Yes. Stream of Consciousness.

I'm finding myself in a garden of apple trees, dancing around every sleeping sunflower, trying to touch the silver moonlight. I'm listening to Gospel music and trying to reach your spirit. Do you remember me? You took my dreams away. I was destroyed by your revolver and my ghost haunting you to find the truth between the stars. It was a hunt late at night from an investigator's eyes. I was collecting bones from unknown humans in the heavy green underbrush, terrifying remains were found on the hillside lot of bones from young girls... jawbones, fractured skulls, clumps of hair, broken fingernails--that told me they were fighting for their lives--eyeballs so frightened that they told me this was something that never could be forgiven. While the dead speak during my work you told another story. You stroke her blond hair, kiss her cherry lips, hold her hand, suck her fingertips with your hungry mouth, push her against the bedroom wall and lick her with your fiery, split tongue, then move down her neck over her silky, swaying ivory breasts. Lips want to kiss her forehead, but in a little moment, you stop… Tick tack tick tack…time stops. With her alabaster hands in metal cuffs, you burn your milky-white sperm into her numb but moist cave. You whisper into her left ear "I need to shatter your head with my steel balls!" She humms in satisfaction, and something knocks her out. A rage only her dead body can express. A fire only her bloody spit can show, and only her soul witnesses a monster's darkest hour. You told me you dragged her between the river and the yellow field, licked her sweet blood from her ears, lips, and eyelashes. Up the road, her head was severed in two … and the road turned red. You were gazing at her blood like it was taunting you, and a demon-loving joy juice was what you left behind. You, who does not look like someone who could tear people to shreds, sat in front of me with a smile that was longing for a kiss on the cheek and so you described how you left the bodies posed in sex acts, a masterpiece with your DNA. In the shadows of death, I don't need to forgive to move on, because when you are finding yourself in a garden of apple trees with your mom's fractured skull in your palms and your life flashing in front your eyes, stir your blood and freeze your heart…

"Mother? Are you there? What can I title this? Please! I need your advice!"

She asks me for advice. That's a good one! She can invite strange men across the world to be partners with her on a case, or send me to chaperone two Huldras in disguise, but she only asks me to give her help with her sick and demented poetry! I suppose this might be a good segue for me to tell her about her next guest, Dr. Paul Balder, V. She can't see me, even with her powers of shapeshifting, speaking with dead spirits, and conferencing with human demons. I *will* give her a title for her poem.

Oh, my dear, I don't know. What about 'Who is the Devil in the Garden?' Or 'Eve's Demon Lover?'

She smiles and looks up, even though my voice is inside her head.

"Yes! I like 'Eve's Demon Lover.' Thank you, Mother. I hope you weren't offended by my reference to you."

Of course not! I can plainly see who this demon is. The same werewolf who murdered me, Mr. Hans Wortle, who is now the Oslo public gymnasium Physics teacher, all pacified with drugs, to keep his rather peculiar tastes at bay--if the full moon will please excuse my expression this once. My goodness! How prescient of me. It is a full moon this evening. How romantic!

"Mother, you know me so well, even though you deserted me at my most vulnerable age. I'll use your title, and I thank you for it. Perhaps we *are* getting closer."

This is my chance to tell her about Dr. Balder. *My dear, have you visited your ladies lately? You were saying how much fun you had with them after that little girl was calling you the other day. I thoroughly enjoyed being their escort. You should really visit them today and find out about the fun they had with the Huldrekall lovers. Perhaps you yourself can experience such bliss. One never knows who might visit you. You told me the leader was quite enamored of you in your Huldra form.*

She's smiling. A good sign. She looks up, fluffs her long blonde hair, and her thick eyebrows rise, in one of her curious poses, her breasts beneath her powder blue detective suit rising and falling.

"Why yes. I was wondering what they experienced. Ever since that case with the girl, my mind has been everywhere else but my sexual affairs. Even Dr. Seagraves was beginning to come on to me, which is not proper. Although, he now knows about me and my supernatural proclivities. I suppose I could use a little adventure again. The best sex I've ever had was with Norse creatures. I cannot be impregnated, as I have a human spirit. This is the best birth control one can have, right?"

She laughs, and I know I have convinced her. Dr. Balder will be there to meet her, and his son informed me that his father will show her a very good time. *I'm so happy for you, Astrid! You must tell me all about it when you return. I will give you complete privacy in these matters.*

My daughter stands up, and I can see her eyes begin to get that dreamy look she always gets whenever she's ready to transition into one of her creatures. I really don't know how many she can become, but I do know her grandfather's curse had a lot to do with it. I wonder what gave him that curse power?

She stands at the door, and when she opens it, I can see it's a beautiful day in March, no snow, as it has melted, and the wind is light, as it gently blows my daughter's hair and skirt freely about. She is so beautiful, and she is artistic. I love her so much more when she loses her maudlin depression.

Enjoy yourself in our beautiful Norway, my dear! May Odin protect you!

Of course, I will be with her on her little tryst. I just wanted her to believe she was going to have privacy. Loki needs my information to give him his own libidinous enjoyment. How can I miss out on this? My mind has urges of its own, after all!

With my spiritual insight, I can also hear what my daughter is thinking as she makes love. What a contrast! Her naked, strong, and vibrant identity as a Huldra, and her inner passion as a woman of thirty-eight. If only I could be part of this miracle. As they say in the spirit world, "No body, no fun."

After she transforms into her Huldra aspect, Lily is looking up into the sky, as she walks barefoot along the path to the waterfall where the Huldra clan live. The brilliant full moon is rising, above the forest line, and now I understand my daughter's trepidation. She remembers how I was killed!

Perhaps she believes Hans Wortle will be lurking about. However, as a Huldra, with great speed and her sharp wooden back spines, I doubt even a psychotic school teacher could do her much harm.

Unless he were an actual werewolf. He was salivating and raging so much when he stabbed me, I never really got a good look at his total appearance. He may have been a real werewolf, come to think of it. Oh well. Life is full of its little surprises. That's what makes it enjoyable.

My daughter as a Huldra in the glorious wonderland of the woods is a breathtaking experience. She can smell the pines and elders, and the frosty air bites at her lips as she steps through the brush toward her rendezvous with a lover she's never met. Not only has she been chaste for over year now, but she has never made love with one of her "people," as she often calls them. Why?

She tells me she believes she is connected to them on a deep level, deeper than the souls we have as humans. This frightens her, and she hasn't attempted to be intimate with any of them, even though she feels it would clean her insides from the blood and the gore that fill her human fantasies every night, especially during the months of the midnight sun.

I am so happy she is doing this! She is now at the clearing near the waterfall, and as I look out toward the mountain which juts up into the sky beside the forest, I look down into the canyon below, filled with dark trees that seem to call you from the heights to meet them in a passionate embrace below. The ledge just beneath this waterfall still is very high above, and I fear for my darling daughter.

I can hear her asking the new mothers, who have already had their children, how the sex was with the Huldrekalls, who they at first believed were attacking them. They were busy doing what Olga did with Marilyn, the murderer of her rapist uncle: trading their babies in for a human baby.

The foxtails disappear, as well as the pointed ears, and their babies look very human when they are traded. In return, they raise their human babes to become new Huldras, breathing into them under the magic waterfall with the divine spirit of Odin.

This makes them into the temptresses, the forest women of the night, or the male Huldrekalls, the underground raging black demons. They both come upon unwary travelers, campers, and photographers, and take them captive.

What do they do to these humans—either male or female—does it depend upon their sexual needs? They ravish them, of course, and then they push them off the cliffs, or send them spiraling down from the waterfall ledge, watch them careen through the air, screaming, their bodies falling, until they dash into bloody pulps against the rocks below.

Then, as a clan, they hold hands around a campfire and sing praises to the men, the Huldrekalls, and to the great Viking and Pagan God, Odin. The answering shrieks in the night from their lovers below make them moist in their vaginas, and they have multiple orgasms, without the men, without their touch, and without a care in the world!

"Why do you have orgasms without them?" Lily asks, as she has never pursued this line of intimate questioning before.

"Huldrekalls are like cats—they have barbs on the sides of their penises. To become impregnated is to be tortured. We never want this again, to scream in pain, so we imagine the experience alone.

We have such fantastic imaginations, we can feel the hard, yet soft outside penis, stroking the insides of our uteruses. The plunging foments of torment disappear, and we can hold hands and have an ultimate Huldra communal orgasm! We gain power and strength to protect our woods from invasion by these humans of pollution, war, and death. Huldras above, Huldrekalls below—the way we prefer it!"

The call comes from beneath the waterfall. It's not the same call as before. Not the piercing, enraged battle cry of the underground, black demons. This voice is much gentler, soothing to the ear, like a strong wind racing through the canyons below, calling you down to your death, perhaps, but still mixing with the raging waters of passionate release all around them.

Her fifteen sisters' pointed ears perk up in unison. They have never heard of such a mating call. My daughter is intrigued, even with her personal taste for violent love, skulls, and blood, she gazes out toward the waterfall, about two hundred meters from their campsite, near the cliff's edge.

The birds and insects seem to chant along with his voice, as he calls out behind the immaculately white froth of the falling waters. What is behind that white mask, they all seem to ask?

When her sisters begin to run toward the call, falling, pushing, and shoving one another for a lead, Astrid Lily knows she must fight to earn her reward. She strikes out, as if she were a rugby player, her head down, pile-driving through these fox-tailed women, her sisters in form only, who are in love with a new experience.

First one, then another, go sprawling, legs splayed helplessly akimbo, twisting, and rolling on the forest floor. And my Lily runs on! Soon she passes them all, and she makes one final push on the lead Huldra, and pulls her tail for good measure, sending the femme fatale gasping and spitting, as she runs for cover into the woods to the left.

Finally, my daughter is at the ledge, and she delicately climbs out onto the mountain's precipice above the crashing waters below. She never looks down, as she gingerly steps under the white, frothing curtain to experience what is behind it.

I can't stand it, of course, so I float over to them, peering behind the curtain to watch. I have seen and done most every sex position in the Hindu Kama Sutra.

I have sucked, licked, kissed, and loved probably every inch of the human body, but I am not prepared for what I now can see, hear, and experience. Yes, and I want to taste it and touch it, but I have no such power in my spiritual existence to do so.

He stands eight feet tall, the same as the others, the black ones. But he is white as the snows of Norway, and his white hair falls in curly rivulets to his muscular shoulders, which are gleaming with moonlight from the full radiance above them. My goodness! I am a spirit, and my virtual vagina is getting wet just seeing this monster of love!

And his tongue! It is forked as well, but as she steps under the canopy of the falls, she reaches out to its soft and pulsating rhythm, as each forked prong is smooth, bloody red, and engorged, like two separate penises ready to probe into her cave of earthly delights.

Can I withstand this? Does Dr. Balder have this ability to shape into such a figure of masculine strength and beauty? *Min Gud*! I instinctively reach down to caress myself, but there's nothing, and I feel immediately crestfallen, as if I want to fall into those waves below!

Such passionate insinuation! Those two probes begin to twist in the air, the spray making them moist and ready, and I can hear my daughter swoon as they visit her between the legs.

Yes, I have experienced a male fist and his rubbing tongue upon my clitoris, but this is an entirely new level of sexual passion. Lily becomes the writhing, snake-like creature, her head falling back against the cliff, her legs quivering, as these two forks in the road to Oz explore her, devour her, in and out, then one of them twirling in the air above her arching body, encircling her neck, and squeezing it, as she screams out her first of what must be fifteen consecutive orgasms!

If all her nightmares of bloody, smiling skulls, violent killers, and demonic lovers don't disappear, then my daughter is sick beyond recovery. This Huldrekall of passion howls at the moon, as his own huge penis rises to greet Lily's mouth, and she responds, lowering her head, as if she's a little girl taking her first pagan communion with nature.

But this nature makes her salivate and gush with release, as her full lips encircle his engorged manhood as if her lips were also squeezing pythons of passion. This sensual motion, the rhythmic dynamic, the smell of hot bodies in love, the feel of their moist joy under the falling waters into nature's abyss. It's breathtaking!

When his twelve inches of Huldrekall passion enters her, I believe I can hear her thank heaven for the first time in her life. She rocks to his rhythmic thrusts, as if she is losing her mind under this waterfall, and perhaps she is. Her face is contorted in ecstatic bliss, as the two tongue prongs enter her from the rear, and she yelps with surprise, so loudly, I can hear the echoes across the canyons below.

After he ejaculates, a spouting gush of white semen across her spiny back, and onto her heaving breasts in front, he does not stop. He kisses her entire body with slow, passionate swirls of his probes and licks every drop of his and her love potion from both of their bodies.

Finally, as the moon is now a much smaller, glowing, full-faced, white witch, above them in the night, he picks her up into his brawny arms, cradles her exhausted head against his broad, hairless chest, and walks out from behind the raging torrent of the waterfall. I see them as they coo to each other, still working their pouting lips, savoring with drowsy eyelids the passion of moments before.

As he carries her to her sisters, I can hear his baritone voice as he sets her amongst her sisters. The others are awe-struck at his image, and their imaginations must be giving them additional orgasms as they stare at his forked, fat, and probing tongue and Herculean physique.

"When she wakes up, please tell her there will be more, in a different place, in a different way, and with even more passionate creatures. I am much obliged to you all. The night of passionate release becomes you, ladies. I salute you, in Odin's name!"

As my daughter sleeps, he creeps off into the forest, his broad back and shoulders moving with panther-like grace, and the earth below him is never disturbed. To me, he's a gift of loving release to my daughter and to her nightmares of hideous experiences. I know I am now working for the right man!

CHAPTER THIRTEEN: THE SEDUCTION

July 2022, Oslo, Norway.

I don't see my "partner" until summer. After our trip to see Edvard Grieg's Museum in Troldhaugen, what the hell she's doing is beyond my scope of imagination. So, we again became "virtual" buddies on the Internet.

Me, hunched down inside my hotel room at The Thief, afraid to open my window shades for fear one of her "creatures" will be there. I'm a fucking military man, born and raised to live life according to structure, plans, and ZEN REALITY! This woman has cast a spell on me, and I'm not going to escape.

So, I leave my lonely room at the first sign of spring. I even start whistling, as I throw on my blue sports jacket, matching slacks, and my press badge. My anchor to San Diego is my pair of navy-blue Nikes. Grieg's music sounds appropriate, as he wrote that piece about spring beginning.

However, I prefer "In the Hall of the Mountain King," as my life is becoming exactly like Mickey Mouse, "Sorcerer's Apprentice" inside the magician's castle. I really don't know what's real and what's imagined anymore.

The Oslo streets have changed. People are looking backwards at others as they do their daily chores. I decide to visit the local journalist's pub, as there's one in every town in the world. This one's across from the Royal Palace, near my hotel, called "Queen Bee."

I don't smoke, but the smell of unfiltered nicotine grabs my lungs with its powerful, pungent odor as I walk inside. There in the back is the table I need to visit. I can hear my language being spoken! It's a miracle already. I'm tired of Lily's emails and messages about how she's "on the case, hunting down Balder's pals, and using her kid killer, the new Huldra, Marilyn Southbine, as an infiltrator and spy."

Lily even says she's miraculously found romance in her life again! That's just dandy. What about me? Do I take one of her trolls out for a night on the town? Get him drunk. Perhaps he'll put out.

These four look like working journalists. Beer in the steins, smokes blazing, and jaws working.

"Excuse me, but do any of you know why these folks are acting so paranoid outside?" I stick my thumb out and point back to the streets behind the swinging doors of the pub.

With journalists, it's aways the same. No matter how stoned, drunk, or tired, they are always up on the latest news that affects humanity. It's no different with these four. Munchkin in granny glasses, tall drink of water with a plaid Tam O'Shanter, woman with tombstones for eyes, and the one who addresses me, a fat guy of about sixty, with caterpillar eyebrows. My generation. He scowls at me, and points his beer stein, as if I have just returned from a Voyager mission.

"You mean the new Peter Lorre pederast mission to clean-up Norway of flashers, streakers, pedophiles, and peeping toms?" He says this in one breath without a smile. Reminds me of myself in my better sarcastic moments with Lily.

"Nice to meet you. My name's Martin. Are they after dudes whose name begins with an M? Oh, not that! I'm old enough to remember that movie, my friend. The thugs in 1931 Berlin mark poor Pete with the white chalk letter and things turn to shit for him after that. Is that what you mean?"

He smiles this time. "Yeah, you might say that, Martin. Balderdash—his majesty Paul Balder, V, of Valhalla Castle and Titan Energy—got the law passed in Norway. Anybody caught showing his or her privates in public, or even if they get caught displaying junk inside their own houses or cars, can be arrested, and put on a list that's published on the Web. Guess what? Balder, as it so happens, also owns the holographic device that will mark the letter 'M' virtually on the perp's back. Any collusion, of course, or suggestion of impropriety aimed at Dr. Balder, so sayeth the editors in the media, shall not be included in your story."

Tam O'Shanter pipes up. Yes, he does have a Scot's brogue. "So, if you're pissed, and the old wanker's hangin' out a bit, the fuzz can put both you and your wanker away!"

Miss Good Ship Lollypop chimes in with, "Women have no wankers, nor penises, so it's a case of reverse discrimination as well. I'm a feminist, but I must empathize with men on this one. Unless we have a dildo or our friendly little vibrators, we won't get hung with the upgraded scarlet letter, apologies to Nathaniel Hawthorne."

It's fun talking to fellow souls of yellow journalism. Discussing this stuff with Lily is like talking about fishing with a cat. My turn to grin. "Sounds about par for the course. Yellow journalism lives, even up in the frozen north."

It's now my chance to inquire about my partner, even if I can feel my head exploding inside with worry.

"Say, do any of you know what Lily Orkidedatter is doing for the police? I'm writing a feature article for my San Diego paper, and I hear she's a bit of a medium and psychologist who interviews psycho killers and their victims." Like a Zen Buddhist monk, I blow it out with one breath: Nirvana.

Munchkin Granny picks up the ball on this one. "Yeah, I just did a story on her. Strange woman. And I use the word judiciously. I got photos of all the country folks who use her to get rid of their evil spirits and her talks with dead family members. She can allegedly, so they say, tell police where to find dead murder victims around these lovely parts. I even interviewed folks who live outside Oslo, next to her grandfather, Sebastian's old farm. They told me both she and he were cursed. They mostly say she's a good Witch of the North. Who knows? I got my money for the story."

This is very interesting. "So, what's up with Lily and Balder? Any connection?"

Old guy takes a swig and puts his pudgy fingers under his chin to muse. "Yeah. There might be. Orkidedatter's mother was a hooker in downtown Oslo. That killer named Hans Wortle stabbed her to death. I did some investigating years ago. It seems the grandfather, Sebastian, liked to import prostitutes to keep him from getting bored after feeding the chickens and milking the cows all day."

I smile, visualizing Lily milking a cow naked, with her tattoos, as she waves her magic wand, making the cow's tits pour the white stuff into the pail on their own.

"Same rumors about Balder. Recently, many big wigs have landed at the airport but haven't been seen again in any of the hotels. Balder looks like Thor from those Marvel movies, and he gets a ton of pussy. He's been employing a lot of immigrant young women at his new castle digs. I even hear he might be running a secret bordello, or something, inside that castle. So, the connection is the importing of pussy, and gay dicks, if you want to connect any dots."

I frown. "Pretty thin connection, but I'll take it. I know Lily, and she's pretty mum about her past. I do know she's been abused by the system and has post-traumatic stress. She now seems to be coming out of it, for some reason, so I was wondering if this Balder guy has anything to do with the happy face smile emojis I've been getting from her lately."

It's the young lady's turn to smile. "Women aren't always the sex fiends you guys make us out to be, you know, Dr. Seagraves. Yes, I know you're working with her. Iraq War vet. Teacher and crime reporter. I even know you were raped. You wrote that letter online raging about the Supreme Court hearings of Trump's appointment, right? I'm very proud to know you. I was also molested as a kid."

It's now time for me to leave. My face is red, and I want to talk to Lily some more about her grandfather and her mother, Ingrid. I know she's interviewing a serial killer today at the police headquarters.

"Thank you, but I must be off. You've been more help than you'll ever know."

They nod at me and go back to their smoking, drinking, and solving the world's problems, which is the typical life of a journalist.

The sun hits my eyes as I open the swinging doors and begin the trek to my destination. Oslo is God's country. If "god" were a demonic and horny Odin with a son, Hod, who's blind, evil, and the dude of darkness. Just Lily's type.

***

It takes me nine minutes by Uber Black to get to the Police Station at Grønlandsleiret 44. They're called the Politiet, and they serve about eight other stations throughout the greater Oslo districts. They're quite different in their methods than in the United States, as I stated before, especially their crime fighting limitations concerning weapons.

Also, according to Lily, they're much more into the psychological side of questioning suspects and victims. In the States, we often use the good cop and bad cop routines in their various ways. Here it's usually good cop, better cop, and psychoanalysis.

When I show the desk officer my press credentials and passport, and mention that Lily Orkidedatter invited me to observe her questioning of a suspect, his face lights up like Bozo the Clown, and he even speaks half-assed English. I find this is often the case in European countries, as English has been learned because of all the tourists and the emphasis on serving the public—especially the paying public—to gain status and revenue.

"Please go to end of hall. Turn left. Room door say *Spøringsrom*. Lily be there soon. Have drink!" He laughs.

I nod and start down the hall. Several patrol officers nod at me, wearing their sky-blue shirts, black slacks, and black caps, with the "Politi" badges on their sleeves, showing the golden Royal Lion of Norway. Now I know why Lily wears her powder-blue business suits to work. So, she can fit in.

Inside the Interrogation Room, there's a huge photo on the wall of a court officer cuffing the Utøya Island shooter, Anders Behring Breivik, so I assume it's at his inquest. Whenever I look at these killers, I always remember that quote about the Nazis by Hannah Arendt, at the Eichmann trial in Jerusalem. "They are banal. Someone you might meet every day," she said. "Eichmann was a clerk, who fell into his job, not understanding any Nazi philosophy."

On the main wall, filling up about a four-foot by seven-foot space, is a one-way mirror, I can see into the interview room. Same as we have, but the chairs inside are plush and comfortable looking.

I keep remembering what Lily told me about her mother's wolfman killer, Hans Wortle, and his accommodations. Keep the killer happy, I suppose, is the Norway way. Especially when the victim is only a prostitute.

I get some coffee from the pot on a table on the right side of the room and pour it into a Styrofoam cup. At least it's strong. The stuff they usually have in the States' police rooms tastes like old testicle sacks marinated in bleach.

I can hear commotion coming from the microphones inside the interrogation room. It's Lily who enters in her blue suit. She has a manila folder and a legal pad with her, and she sits down in the chair facing the chair on the other side of the three by five table. She seems calm, and she takes out a pencil from her top jacket pocket and sets it on top of the pad.

We wait about five minutes, and the door opens again. Two brawny policewomen escort another person between them into the room. The prisoner person is over six feet tall. I say "person" because I don't know the sex. Until she speaks.

The voice is female, but it has a gravely soprano sound. The cops have supplied me with an auto-translator, so I can hear the interview in English. The prisoner says, "Can you turn that refrigerator off? It's like ice in here."

She's in plainclothes, a tan skirt and black blouse, as they don't require orange or other jumpsuits here. Her brown hair is short, buzz-cut on the sides, and this designer mane has lightning bolts shaved into her skull, the same ones on the collars of the Nazi S.S. She has plastic twister cuffs, and ankle cuffs, so she duck-walks until she's finally at the chair, and the two guards push down on her shoulders, so she collapses into the pillowed chair.

Immediately, the woman's dark brown eyes scan the room like the searchlight on a prison guard tower. I can feel her eyes on mine when she looks at the two-way mirrored wall. It's very creepy. They look through me.

There's something about a female killer that scares me more than the males. I remember Aileen Wuornos, in Florida, as I wrote a story about her. She was so self-righteous about defending herself from "those fucking predator men," you almost believed her argument about carrying her gun in self-defense.

This woman seems to have the same pugnacious attitude as Wuornos. She has acne all over her face and neck, and she wipes her mouth as best she can with the backs of her wrists and rivets her eyes on Lily, while keeping up a constant drumming of her fingers' black nails upon the table. I can see her right leg bouncing up and down.

"Miss Ingunn Dahl. You are twenty-five years old. You live at 22 Helga Vaneks vei, Mortensrud?" Lily establishes the identity of the suspect.

Dahl grunts and nods in the affirmative.

"You were found gazing out of the window, holding a bloody knife, inside the room with the prostitute. She was stabbed twenty-seven times, and your fingerprints are on the weapon. Why did you stab her?" Lily establishes the crime scene, and her gaze is steady.

Dahl smiles, her purple lips curling up to show nicotine-stained teeth. She leans forward, keeping up the tapping on the table. "Orkidedatter. Don't you know who I really am?"

Lily returns the smile. "When did you first think about killing someone? Please be specific."

"I was created to kill. Don't you know? I am your hidden doppelganger. When you go to sleep, you are me. I slurp blood up from the cuts. I stab your victims. I am you. Lily Orkidedatter. I create your poetry. I should be famous. Not you!" Another smile, and this time she holds her gaze on Lily, and she stops her nervous finger tapping and foot bouncing.

When I see Lily's breathing pace increase, and her chest begins to heave, I remember. The online troll she told me about who said she loved Lily's macabre poetry. She said she wanted to become Lily. Is this the same woman?

"How do you know me? I don't know you," Lily says, her voice rising at the end of the last sentence.

"Loki sends me. He sends me everywhere. I kill so he can enjoy my murders in his spirit world. Bad girls and bad boys are my specialty. You are a very bad girl, Lily. Your mother is a whore. Your grandfather cursed you and killed that fox. I am also the soul of that prostitute your grandfather murdered on that dark night in the woods. I came to kill you!" She laughs, a high-pitched laugh that makes the microphone squeal in my ears.

"No. You are a murderer. A serial killer. I have seen dozens of you before. They each have stories they invent. You weave a good nightmare, but I know you are not really who you say you are." Lily seems to be calm again. She writes something on her pad and stands up. "I think that's all for today, Miss Dahl."

The prisoner stands, and she towers above Lily's five feet four inches. "Watch your spiny back, Huldra! I will kill you when you least expect me. Look at that screen. Now! I will soon be out to murder you and become you!"

The woman turns and stares directly at me. No scream. No motion. Just that stare into what Nietzsche calls the "dark abyss."

"We'll get you mental help," Lily says. "Some Librium, perhaps."

The woman raises her cuffed hands and points two forefingers at me. "Why don't you give the old guy Martin a break, Lily? He wants to fuck you so bad he can taste your blood! Just the way I taste you in your dreams!"

When the one-way mirror shatters, I step back. After making spider cracks, the fragments splinter and fall on the floor in front of me. I look up. I can see her eyes, and she can see mine. I have never been as frightened of anybody in my life.

After they take the prisoner out of the room, I meet Lily in the hallway. She is crying, and I take her into my arms. I hold her close to my chest and feel her heart racing and her breathing is rapid and hysterical.

"Lily, I'll protect you. Don't be afraid," I say, kissing her forehead. I want to kiss her lips, but she pulls back. She storms down the hallway, and as she turns back at me, her eyes look like fire has engulfed them. Fire eyes.

My partner, Lily Orkidedatter, I discover later, can't speak. She is dumb, and all I can do is write to her by cell phone message.

CHAPTER FOURTEEN: THE MALDOROR CIRCLE

August 2022, Valhalla Castle.

Marina (Marilyn) and Olga, her surrogate mother, even though they're the same age, are now accepted members of Dr. Balder's chosen few employees. They live and sleep at the plush cottages down the road from Valhalla Castle, where other employees stay when not inside the castle.

These apartments are for single young people, some as young as fourteen and fifteen years of age. The campus has a gymnasium, school rooms, library, a heated Olympic-sized pool, café and restaurant, and a discotheque club since none of them is allowed to go into Oslo to party.

This is fine with the two girls, as they plan to go deeper into the castle than serving as tour guides and performing as actresses in Dr. Balder's commercials for the new law to prevent public masturbation. The recent war in Ukraine has increased business inside the secret part of Valhalla, and both Olga and Marina are meeting with Dr. Balder to be interviewed for a new position.

They both wear the castle's uniform of tight black skirt and blouse, with the Valkyrie patches on their shoulders, with "Balder Valhalla" in Gothic script above the flying and screaming bird women below. Every female employee knows the Valkyrie determines who goes to Odin's Valhalla heaven and who doesn't. The male employees have similar patches, with images of Dr. Balder on the patches.

At midnight, they enter the main portico entrance using the one-time QR Code given to them by Dr. Balder's office to open the doors. This code also operates a panel located behind a statue of King Haakon VII, who famously resisted pressure to abdicate during World War Two, causing the citizens to resist the Nazi occupation. As Marilyn puts her cell phone QR Code up to the king's mouth, the entire wall behind the king opens to the left, and they walk inside.

Marilyn knows it's the way they made love with Dr. Balder, after he met with them that first time, which had secured them this position inside the castle. With their Huldra training, she and her sister knew how to seduce human males, until they become entranced.

Physical movements and athletic dexterity, yes, as this had always been an allure, but when Marilyn and Olga began to sing the chants of the forest primeval and whisper to Balder that he was the most magnificent lover they had ever experienced, the man finally became theirs. He shuddered and climaxed, and as he did this, he shouted inside his castle room, "the Circle of Maldoror! You will work there for me, you wonderful ladies!"

Marilyn knows, this time, it will be different. After they learn what is inside this Circle of Maldoror, they are going to transform into their Huldra forms and murder him. It will be a performance of a lifetime, and they have practiced it for weeks inside their apartment so nothing can go wrong. The witch who saved her, Lily Orkidedatter, will be proud of them and give a Huldra clan celebration and festival by the waterfall.

As they stand next to the stone wall of the inner castle, the two young women fuss with their black hair, touch-up each other's make-up, and then add more French perfume to their wrists and behind their ears. They hear the steps coming down the hall of the fortress section of the castle. It sounds like a soldier, but it's Dr. Balder, wearing the full regalia of a Ninth Century Viking.

His blonde hair falls over his shoulders in curly rivulets. His mountain goat horns adorn the silver helmet, a bear-skin cloak covers his broad chest, a smaller version circles his hips, and his strong, brown legs push him forward like a human bull. Only black combat boots from the Russian Army are modern. His swarthy face bursts into a grin as he reaches them standing under the burning torches on the wall.

"My lovelies! So happy to see you tonight. Come. I will show you the room where I watch." His bulging bicep flexes, and his forearm thrusts forward, the forefinger pointing down the corridor.

They follow him, and Marilyn's heart begins to beat faster in expectation. It's like the way she felt at six, as she marched into her uncle's bedroom, knowing he was not long for this world, clutching her "Hello Kitty" bag of knives to her thin body.

The room looks like a giant network of large computer monitors, seven on the top row, seven on the bottom row. Dr. Balder walks up to each one and boots it on, and as he does so, they can see each of the screens light up, one-by-one, exposing different castle rooms on each of the seventeen-inch computer screens. Their boss beckons them to come forward to get a better look at each screen, and they do so.

"These are the Circles of Maldoror," Dr. Balder says, his baritone confident and strong. "As my son, Loki, says, each room represents the progress of humanity toward total conquest over the weak. The passions begin at our least expensive seven circles, the outside circle of lust rooms. The bottom seven are the most expensive for our clientele. The inner circle of pain. They contain the most original and heinously provocative entertainments of the flesh. I will briefly describe their contents. It will be your job to watch these monitors and clean the rooms after they've finished."

Marilyn's eyes scan quickly over the screens, as each is large and filled with a different décor and characters within them. The activities going on in each make her vagina wet, and she fights the urge to plunge her hand down the front of her skirt.

"Numbers one through seven, going from left to right. Cowboy cell. Ice cream parlor cell. Rock star cell. Boyz in the Hood cell. Nun and Priest cell. Beauty Pageant cell. Gone with the Wind cell."

As Marilyn's eyes take in each screen of the top row, the images flash across her consciousness like a pornographic collection of dreams: saloon whore, squealing, hands on the bed, her skirts hiked over her back, the cowboy eating her pussy voraciously and then thrusting deep with his erection; two coeds in the ice cream parlor, the soda jerk male, spreadeagled upon the countertop, his young loins engulfed with ice cream, hot fudge, nuts, and whipped cream, and his "banana" the main feast for both girls; Guitarist playing wildly on a raised platform, strobe lights cascading across the adoring teen, who is taking off pieces of her clothing, screaming, and throwing them at him; Two young Black men pounding their fists all over the naked body of a white businessman, who is obviously enjoying the pain; A young nun passionately kissing a priest in a hospital bed, her tongue then exploring other parts of his body; Three young ladies in swimsuits, with different countries' names across their banners, dropping their tops and exposing their breasts for the three male judges seated in chairs in front of them; a Southern Belle Scarlet O'Hara being lifted, as she screams, then carried over to the four-poster bed and dropped.

Before Marilyn can catch her breath, Dr. Balder begins describing the bottom row of monitors and their contents:

"Numbers seven through fourteen. Again, from left to right. Lice are nice--so are other curious parasites; Fun times at the bone yard cemetery; Do hermaphrodites really have more fun? Midget and dwarf mania; Fucking up some fags; Zombies and real necromancers; Putin's generals get rewarded."

Moving her dark eyes across these big screens is too much for Marilyn's libido. As she watches what plays out on each screen, she begins to masturbate, frantically, her right-hand thrust beneath her skirt, under her panties, and her head moves, back and forth, as she moans and pants. She doesn't care if Balder sees her. She doesn't care about Olga. All she cares about is that this, at long last, fulfills her inner, demonic world of sensory cravings and violent passions.

A very young nude girl is being covered with millions of lice, and they dart through her scalp, feasting on her blood, as it trickles down the sides of her innocent and lovely face, while three suited onlookers masturbate; in this cell room cemetery, three muscle men, with tattoos all over their bodies, tear open a coffin and expose a dead boy, still bleeding from his torture, and they break off his arms and his legs, and, as the blood spurts all over their tanned bodies, they bugger each other with the child's skeletal parts and lick the blood off the bones; a tall female form, sits on a four-poster bed, masturbating both her vagina and her penis, as three naked and muscular athletes dance to Heavy Metal music under the strobe lights of the cell, their pricks fully erect and filled with passion; little people in an orgy, wearing ballet tutus and tights, as they collide and then tear off their clothing, screaming, as Swan Lake plays, and they make love, male on male, male on female, female on female, moaning and groaning, fondling each other in hundreds of ways, whipping each other until they draw welts; men run in circles around a huge and muscular hooded executioner, their arms flailing wildly, as he whips their backs, legs, and asses, until bloody, with a cracking black bullwhip, and their cocks engorge, as they scream for more, as Little Richard sings his songs; two lovely women, with tattoos all over their naked bodies, are being sliced by the knives of two obese Black men, who drag their feet and have the vacant stares of zombies, they fuck these women as they bleed, licking and slurping at the ladies' bloody tattoos, their portly, dead bodies performing a mechanical thrusting, no emotion, no love, other than the blood-love, and the constant tongue searching for more of the crimson liqueur of demons; three Russian Army generals with three blonde women, blindfolded, naked except for American and Ukraine flags around their pussies, and the generals pull out their pistols from leather holsters, shoot the women in the back of their heads, and then the feasting begins with Wild West Bowie knives, scraping across the dead bodies, the generals licking the blood of their victims off the knives, cutting into their own tongues with both sides of the blades until they scream in passionate release from their mental torture.

"Well, now that you've seen the master viewing control panel, let me escort you to the room in the castle where you'll stay when not working." Dr. Balder smiles as he leads the women out of the room. "I've just had these monitors installed, as we keep expanding our business venture around the world. Although the identities of those you see are already hidden securely, we believe it's best to keep a record and clean the cells. Of course, none of the people in those cells is harmed in any way. Quite realistic, don't you think?"

Marilyn is thinking that anything is now possible. Just like the dream world of sex abusers, who say they can teach and groom children how to love by having sex with them, the way her uncle did, this world of Dr. Balder is providing a rationale for abuse. Even if the people in these cells are CGI or holographic and surreal imposters, she knows these events are happening in some form, somewhere.

Marilyn can't prevent her own dark psyche from masturbating because of abuse and murderous thoughts, but it's time to kill this lying bastard. This is the true purpose of the Huldra, whose revenge upon any evil human animal, who has no restraints or boundaries, is quite proper under Odin's law. Only the Huldra clan lives this way.

The cell is down three doors from Dr. Balder's sleeping quarters. Inside, it is spacious and decorated for the young women with colorful wall photos of the wondrous sights of Norway. Trams climbing to the snow-capped peaks, the green woods, and fjords of the primeval world of Norse mythology, and, naturally, the towering majesty of Valhalla Castle. There are two queen-sized beds with spreads of fox skins and satin pillows with the gold crown of Norway emblazoned upon them.

"There is no clothing storage, I'm afraid," Balder says. "You will receive the same daily uniform as you now wear, cleaned and pressed, from our little robot butlers. We obviously have the latest technologies available in the world."

It's now time for the girls to put their plan into action. Marilyn steps closer to Dr. Balder, gazing up into his ice-blue eyes, her words ready to cover his being with their poetic and symbolic enchantment.

"Dr. Balder, I have written a poem in honor of our transformation. Being inside your secret Circle of Maldoror has changed me forever, as you may have noticed, as I had to please myself in front of you at the viewing monitors."

Marilyn and Olga slowly strip off their black blouses and toss them onto the fox fur bed. Then, they unhook their short skirts, and do the same. They wear no stockings, panties, or bras, so the effect is immediate, and their employer's eyes rove over them, and he licks the lips under his walrus mustache, and he takes off his helmet and places it on the floor, soon followed by the rest of his Viking attire. They stand in the center of the room, naked, feeling the central air conditioning and hearing the piped classical music of Edvard Grieg's "Morning Mood" drift through the air in a springtime fantasy.

Marilyn, her breast nipples perky, and her vagina already wet, steps closer to him, until she can feel the heat from his body.

"I call this poem 'Metamorphosis,' for reasons that will be quite obvious." She then reads the following poem, her voice melodic and passionate, her breasts rising with the breath of each line of desire:

> *I have danced on the devil's bones and*
> *undressed the winter moon.*
> *I have cried blood drops and created*
> *masterpieces from voices in my head.*
> *When my mind fades into a dark place,*
> *crawling and fighting up and down,*
> *in the shadows of death, and*
> *my heart is singing soft lullabies to my demons,*

I'm not touchable, and it's not making me
into a monster,
but I'm rising in the fire like a delicate,
wicked beast, to entwine frozen orchid petals
only to show my heart of glass,
my sparkling tears,
a shattered soul so easy to break...
But I died and was reborn as a virgin, and
I still dance in blue to be created
-anew-
on a blank canvas...

As she reads, she can watch the effect of her words. His penis begins to engorge with blood half-way through her poem, and it is at full mast by the time she says "anew." She nods solemnly at her partner, and they transform before him, born again, into their Huldra forms.

The plan is succinct. Performing like two bookends, each young Huldra turns her razor-sharp and spiny back toward Dr. Balder. With a ferocious war whoop, their pointed ears flat against their heads, and their practiced and acrobatic bodies ready, they spring up and into the air, aiming to crush the tall man between them like a browned turkey breast between two pieces of killer bread.

Another scream penetrates the walls of stone, and the girls' bodies are frozen in time and space. Dr. Balder stands, immobile, between them, smiling, as he picks up his helmet and places it over his head of long hair. "Thank you, Loki, for freeing her. Ladies, let me introduce you to my newest employee, Miss Ingunn Dahl."

The six-foot woman enters the room. She looks at the two Huldras held in inanimate suspension from the powers of her witchcraft, and she blows on her hands. She's wearing a new uniform, the same black skirt and blouse as the girls were supposed to wear. However, since Ingunn is a serial killer, who is prone to a non-hygienic lifestyle, her two legs beneath the short skirt are hairy and pock-marked, and her dark eyes are glowing with passionate ecstasy.

"I'll take the mother, and you can have her daughter, Doctor," she says, grinning, her brown teeth showing. "It is good practice for my rendezvous with Lily Orkidedatter, after you've softened her up with your own trysts, of course!"

"Of course!" Balder says, and he moves back to the far side of the room, pulls the strap beneath his chin, and lowers his head. "All right, release her!" he shouts.

Dahl screams once more, and Marilyn falls to the floor, landing on her feet. Before she can react, Dr. Balder runs full speed toward her and gores her breasts with the goat horns on his helmet. The Huldra smashes against the stone wall, blood spurting out of her mouth, the spines in her back inverting to gore her from the back, as the bloody wounds gush forth, spraying down over her waist and into her vaginal cavern. Marilyn's final life blood flows, like a crimson river inside the Huldra woods, in streams of deathly sorrow.

Dahl's next scream drops Olga to her feet, and the tall serial killer, her long-nailed black hands in front of her body, rushes at the short woman. In a final attempt to attack, Olga leaps into the air, but Dahl pulls a ten-inch knife from a black sheath at her waist, and, just as Olga falls, spines-down, to gore the serial killer, Dahl rips upward, thrusting through the spines and into Olga's heart.

Dr. Balder watches, with keen interest, as Ingunn gets on her hands and knees and begins to slurp the gushing blood from Olga's open wound. The employer, pulling his helmet from Marilyn's corpse, licks the blood from the horns, and then steps in to devour huge chunks of bloody red meat from the dead Huldra's stomach.

In the other room, the scream of sexual release comes from Loki's spirit, and the classical music has stopped, drowned out by the exultant wails of all three, inside this Hell on Earth.

However, floating above them, in the rafters of the stone room, is the ghost of Lily Orkidedatter's mother, Ingrid. She recognizes Ingunn Dahl, but she can't recall the exact place where she saw her. What bothers her most is how she can convince her daughter of the innate evil of what has just occurred. Was Dr. Balder the shapeshift creature at the waterfall? How can she prove that these murders of the two Huldras took place? Even now, the evidence is being destroyed, eaten by these two ghouls, in a macabre blood feast.

CHAPTER FIFTEEN: PRINCE HOD

September 2022, Oslo, Norway.

I can't imagine what's wrong with my partner now. She doesn't meet with me for a week, she only texts, and the police say she can't work for them because she can't speak, so she isn't able to interview the psychos and other suspects for them. So, I spend my time in The Thief Hotel, playing online solitaire, writing poetry about Norse monsters, and watching old reruns of *Playboy After Dark* in Norwegian on cable TV. When I hear Bill Cosby say, *Jeg elsker jazzen i kveld, Hef* ("I love the jazz tonight, Hef"), considering recent history, I almost split a gut laughing. Then, in late June, I get this text from her:

Meet me at my cabin. I have something I want to show you. It may change your life.

Change my life? What about hers? I already had my mind blown when I saw her little creature pals at the Grieg Museum. Not to mention the most recent interview with attractive Miss Ingunn Dahl, who vowed to escape and kill my partner and me. What could change *my* life at this juncture? Will we be taken up into the Mother Ship to be probed by Aliens? My mind is open to that, as I've already been screwed over by the military, and now my new adventure on the paranormal funny farm in Norway is at its peak.

As I'm probably the world's original "glutton for punishment," I hire another Black Uber, and he turns out to be an eighty-six-year-old who drives about fifteen miles per hour around mountain roads, and into the valley of death, which I visualize as where Lily's cabin is. I don't speak Norwegian, and he knows no English. I chalk that up to good practice for meeting Lily, who doesn't speak either. To top it all off, it's nine in the evening, and it's still daylight out, and will be for many more hours. My biological clock has turned on my "fight or flight panic mode," and I have yet to see one of Lily's friendly monsters.

As the old man swerves his Prius indelicately onto the winding path leading down to the tree-sheltered retreat of my friend and partner, I come to the astounding realization that I have been wanting to have her sexually and to experience her darkness for my own salvation, as my entire life has been lived in darkness. Lily is the physical and mystical experience I must have to redeem my soul from a living hell. When I try to joke to make her smile, my heart is breaking.

Lily is standing in front of her cabin, and the sun is radiant above the treetops. She's wearing her usual powder blue business suit, but her usually ice-blue irises are glowing and red, and her chest heaves with passionate desire. As I walk up to her, I can smell the luscious beauty of her body, and it mingles with the spine-tingling odors all around us in the wildness of this savage world.

I may be fifty-seven, but I know when a woman is in heat, and I can smell her loins from where I stand. She is even shivering in the summer warmth, as she stares out past the forest greenery, and she points toward the tallest mountain range, near the Russian border, called Rondane. The name sounds like an American hair rejuvenation product. Not very romantic.

She points, with her right index finger, and, as she does so, she reaches with her other hand into the jacket pocket and pulls out two pills and hands them to me, palm up. She then nods at her suit's top pocket, where there's a slip of paper. She wants to me to read it. I extract it and read the following:

Martin, please take these pills. They're potassium iodide tablets. We're going up to the Hall of the Mountain King, and the Russians may try to stop me. They know about Dr. Balder, and they're trying to protect him. Putin might use his tactical nukes. I am going to marry Balder's brother, Prince Hodr, in a ceremony. Once this happens, there will be peace on Earth, and the Baldr Castle, for this is what it truly is, will be cleansed forever. You don't know my culture. The story goes back millions of years. Their father, Odin, was concerned about Baldr, who kept suffering from terrible nightmares. So, Odin traveled to Nifhelm, the land of the dead, where he resurrected a wisewoman and asked her for advice. She told him that Hodr would eventually slay Baldr, so Odin went back to Asgard, not happy about these developments.

I look into my darling Lily's eyes, and they pierce mine with their scarlet glare, like the midnight sun, until I must look away to keep from going blind. I squint at the rest of her paper, gimlet-eyed, and read:

Odin spoke with Baldr's mother, Frigga, who decided to have all the creatures on earth swear an oath not to harm Baldr this way, Hodr could use no weapon against his brother. Unfortunately, Frigga missed her chance to speak with the mistletoe bush. Tricked by Loki, Hodr created an arrow from the mistletoe branch which pierced Baldr's body, killing him instantly. In some stories, it is not an arrow but a spear instead. The death of Baldr at Hodr's hand signified the darkness ruling over the light. As the nights grew longer and colder, the sun faded away each year.

I must marry Hodr. Unless I do so, he will not be able to get the mistletoe branch to create the arrow. We can only kill Dr. Balder with it and nothing else. Come with me, and I will change into the only person who can marry Hodr. I will change your form into a troll, so you can be permitted to observe our wedding and our lovemaking. As a troll, you will become a eunuch, so you can't feel any lust. It's the only way you can be permitted to observe.

I suddenly feel a great compassion for Lily. Her mind has been overworked, and now she's lost sight of what part of existence is real and which part is myth and fantasy. I suppose it's the current fad if one examines life carefully. Most humans have become narcissists. As I follow her, I keep wondering when she'll turn me into a troll and what kind of creature she will become. As she steps off the porch shadows of her cabin, and into the perpetual daylight, she starts shucking her clothes as she walks, in her usual quick-step pace. My ears are growing, and I can feel them. Yes, they're pointed, the same way I was transformed by Lily on our trip to the Grieg Museum woods at Troldhaugen.

Her jacket comes off first, and as she drops it to the loamy forest floor, I can feel my nose begin to enlarge and widen in the middle of my face. The skirt comes next, which she flings with abandon against an elder tree's bark. I watch her thighs and sweet buttocks, as they undulate, and I get hard. Her tattoos are now exposed, each one a frozen memory she has about her dark life of examining and questioning the lives and deeds of killers, pedophiles, and rapists.

As a naval officer, I saw so many sailors and marines getting their tattoos: screaming eagles, globes and anchors, Iraqi damsels in chadors, coiled snakes, naked belly dancers, tear drops, Disney characters, weapons of all kinds, all carved upon their young bodies during their assortment of liberty celebrations on land in Baghdad. I always enforced the regulation which said, "no tattoo will be seen below a jumper sleeve." One Machinist Mate from New Jersey told me he would "get me after the war," when I disciplined him, so I had the kid court-marshaled out of the service.

However, on the night before I was given my psychiatric medical discharge, I was in San Diego, far from the war. I took a prostitute escort with me, as I was quite inebriated, into a tattoo parlor past Market Street, and I pulled out a drawing I'd created during my two tours of duty during the Iraq War. I handed it to the young, long-haired Cahuilla Tribal member, and I told him I wanted a tattoo of that illustration needled into my chest.

As Lily glances back at me, my sport coat and shirt miraculously fall from my torso, exposing my only tattoo, and I am ashamed she can now see me. She can see my gray chest hairs and sagging breasts, but, most of all the image of the three Iraqi children being blown apart by an incoming laser-guided bomb from an F-14B Tomcat, long-range Navy fighter jet. My political purpose was to make a statement about the supposed accuracy of our most technologically efficient weapons, which often "go astray" of their target to kill people, which we call "collateral damage."

This, I see on the news in 2022, with some satisfaction, is now happening to the Russians, at war with Ukraine, and it's occurring at an even more frequent rate. When my medical officer saw this tattoo during my required medical check-up at the BOQ, he reported it, and I was, quite ironically, given my psychiatric discharge, and my Congressional appointment was negated.

Even with all the carnage and victims Lily sees, on a weekly basis, she has no tattoo exhorting violence of any kind. This is what makes me ashamed, and so I cross both my forearms against my chest, as I feel my legs and arms begin to form into knobby, hairy, and elongated appendages, stretching my torso, until I stand over eight feet tall, marching behind her into the forest primeval. The fur on my chest has also grown over my tattoo, so I am quite pleased about that.

I see my partner, striding ahead of me, and she is also beginning to physically transform. Upon her back, on the shoulders, the black buds erupt, which grow into two enormous bat wings, and at that very moment, I can feel my penis and testicles begin to shrink, slowly at first, but then faster, until they are tiny and useless little peas in a hairy pod beneath a worm so small that it looks like a parrot's beak. In fact, when I reach down to touch it, it is quite hard, not in an erection, but petrified by Lily's magic. I remember. *I must become a eunuch to participate in this wedding.*

By the time we reach the giant lake between the two mountains, we are both transfigured into our mythological forms. I once explained to Lily that there is no "matter," in the sense that everything we see, when reduced to its contents, is made of more space, and that what we see, in so-called "reality" is nothing more than molecules moving at such high speed that they appear to be "hard." In other words, a table is simply energy moving so fast that it looks and feels like it's "hard," but it's actually energy shifting at light speed.

I told her I knew a teacher in college, a physicist, who believed in this concept of matter being mostly space so much so that he wore padded elevator shoes to keep from falling through the floor. I now understand that Lily's shapeshifting is no more than an ability to move the energy inside the shapes she imagines so that it changes into whatever she wants the shape to be. Call it "magic" or a witch's curse, or the reality of physics; it makes no difference. I am now an eight-foot, hairy, Norwegian troll, with pea-shaped balls and a parrot beak dick. And my darling Lily? As she climbs ahead of me, onto the last ledge going up into the colossal cavern of this mountain, has completely transformed into Hela, the ancient Goddess of the Underworld. She is now ready to wed her husband, the Prince of Darkness, Hodr.

Can I describe such a transformation without losing touch with reality? My sense of humor has abandoned me, as I know Lily is lovesick. She is infused with such an intense desire that I can see her body tremble, as her muscular thighs drive her upward, and the sharp antlers growing out of her long, raven hair, are not "matter," either, as they wave in the mountain winds like probing strobes of passion. She is strong, yes, and the giant, black-bladed spear she holds in her right hand serves as a hiking stick. Her black bear coverlet adorns her murky armor and shapely torso, and she lets out a Viking war cry as she reaches the summit.

As I reach the ledge, I am stumbling, my huge hands and wooly head shake, from side-to-side, with exasperation at my clumsiness.

What I see is a wonderous scene out of Lily's book of Scandinavian folklore.

A gigantic, pearl-white human skull, as large as a two-story building, sits in the shadows of the cave, as five waterfalls of steaming, liquid fire cascade down the mountain's cavern walls, as if Hell itself has been raised up, out of a deep and dark pit of anguish, just for this single day's appearance within these lofty heights of Odin and his sacred realm of Valhalla. Valkyries—screaming and winged harpies with lances, armor, helmets and spears--glide in lazy loops above us, in the dark cave's rafters, and my sense of humor returns. If this is The Hall of the Mountain King, then it must be the wedding. I put my giant hands to my mouth and shout at Lily, who has now stepped inside the portal into the darkness.

"Lily! Are these flying women eunuchs also? Or are you giving them a special dispensation because they call the shots about who gets into heaven? Huh?"

The woman who turns to stare down at me, however, is not my Lily. Her two eyes are red coals, and, as her mouth opens, I can see the sharp vampire canines and a black forked tongue. Her voice bellows at me so loudly that I can feel its heat upon my homely troll face.

"Silence, worm! Hodr approaches!"

Is this truly the marriage of Hell in Valhalla? Will the final battle of Ragnarök happen once they are joined? What about the Russians? And Dr. Balder's Valhalla Castle? Serial killer Ingunn Dahl? Are they real? Shapes shift into place, and they create a new reality, a reality where my partner, the orphan, the sex-crazed medium and witch, Astrid Lily Orkidedatter, who works for the Oslo police on her off days, now becomes the keeper of the eternal pit of darkness. She's here to marry this guy Hodr to ensure that the battle at the end of the world can come off without a hitch. No, nothing crazy about that. It's just a fluke of chance. Like all human thoughts and imaginings throughout time, right? If there *is* such an apparition called "time."

As I lumber into the shadows of the cave, I can feel the deadly silence all around. The Valkyries stop flying and cling to the sides of the cavern walls like frightened bats. One of them lands too close to the river of fire and singes her wings. Lily, as the Goddess Hela, raises her arms and stares into the pitch-dark abyss, about ten meters away, a huge portal in the side of the grotto. From out of this smokey darkness comes a man being escorted by two black wolves, who snap and snarl as they move, their muscled haunches and legs straining, their bodies close to the ground in a predatory posture.

This man is obviously blind, cloaked in a huge wolf skin, over his dark armor, but his muscular frame is lithe, and he walks with a feminine gait, his hips twisting, his shoulders swiveling like Joe Dalessandro, in one of Andy Warhol's gay movies. He has long black hair, but his one affectation is a crimson silk scarf tied around his forehead. I expect Lou Reed to start singing "Walk on the Wild Side," as he enters. The shades he wears are black, and as he moves out into the center of the wedding chapel, I can sense a speech coming on, and I am not disappointed.

"Do you know how much tail I'm giving up by doing this? This isn't a rhetorical question, Hela, this is for real, baby doll! We blind fellows get so much sex because women think of us as soothsayers and magicians who can see into their souls. Besides, what woman doesn't understand that a blind guy won't make any sarcastic remarks about her appearance in bed? Huh?"

His deep laugh shakes the sides of the cave. Two Valkyries fall from their perches and must flutter back again, like two canaries, holding on with their trembling hands. I can't help but giggle at his folksy wisdom, either, as I happen to be the only other male. Wait. Yes. The wolves don't count, but sadly, I am male in mind only.

"Lord Hodr, we must proceed with the marriage. Your brother is attempting to take-over the world! We must find the mistletoe bush to create the arrow that kills him." Lily's voice sounds melodious, sweet, and pleading. Why doesn't she use that tone with me occasionally? I always feel like she's going to duck out of the room to her next interview with a pedophile or serial killer. That does wonders for your ego, believe me.

"Hold your forked tongue, Miss Hela. I'm not finished. Men, on the other hand, as lovers, care much more about my appearance. Subsequently, they are more difficult to get into the sack." Hodr pulls up the wolf skin around his waist to show his package. "However, they can usually be convinced with a bit of animal behavior. But now I won't have any of my free spirit! What is a brother to do?"

Hodr's walk becomes a mincing step of gay pride, his hands and wrists waving, his buttocks swaying, as he prances over to stand next to the yawning mouth of the giant white skeleton head. He turns toward Hela and smiles.

"Woman, we obviously don't need any religious service in The Hall of the Mountain King. Let's get it on, baby doll. Come see what daddy's got for you. I see you brought your troll doll. He *is* a big boy! Can't we have a threesome?"

"Hodr, you know very well, from this moment on, nothing can come between us or Ragnarök cannot happen. My troll is a eunuch, and so are the Valkyries."

Lily finally answers my question, albeit not directly. Her blazing eyes, I see, are staring down at her groom's waist, so she is totally captivated. I watch her vamp canines flash and her black tongue slither as her mouth opens. Her steps are purposeful and strident, and she turns toward me just as she reaches the mouth entrance to the skull face. "What are you waiting for? Come!" She roars at me, and I lumber on over and peer inside.

There are hundreds of wolf skins on the floor of the skull room, and Hodr's two giant wolves move to one corner, lay down peacefully, and go to sleep. Their master, however, doesn't have sleep on his mind. He moves on his bride at once, pulling off her helmet of gyrating horns and tossing it aside. Next comes her bearskins and dark armor, exposing her brown, naked skin beneath. Unlike Lily, her Hela form has no tattoos. Just a silky-smooth skin that resembles the underside of a Black Mamba snake. Just two drops of venom can kill a human.

When she's finally nude and panting, her large breasts heaving, she attacks Hodr and has him naked in twenty seconds, and her forked tongue engorges with blood to swell and encircle her groom's twelve-inch erection.

I've had some blowjobs in my life, but this is phantasmagorical and quite delicious to watch. Nothing like supernatural beings to improve humanity's way of doing things, I always say. Wait. I've never seen anything like *this* before. How can I say that? Hodr rips off his shades and stares down at what she's doing to him. His pupils are blind, but they are still present, and their irises are turning as crimson as Lily's are. I suppose his diet of human sex hasn't been this good, either. His handsome face contorts into an ecstatic grimace, and he begins to howl. Yes, just like a wolf. And his two seeing-eye dogs momentarily perk their ears, but soon fall back to sleep. Been there, done that, they seem to be saying.

Yes. Hodr is now becoming what Jim Morrison called her "backdoor man," as a reward for her attention a few moments before. He raises her two buttocks to meet his thrusts, and Lily begins to howl. Doesn't she have any respect for her departed mother, Ingrid? The poor woman was stabbed to death by a wolf man, for heaven's sake! Nope. She still howls like a beast. Then comes some flipping over, and pile-driving movements that make me believe my earlier tale about matter not existing is a crock of doo-doo. I have never seen such action in sex before, and I have watched my share of porno, believe me. These two are sucking, spreading, fondling, and licking every part of the body, and this happens at lightning speed, so that it all appears to my naked eyes to be a solid force of impenetrable union. When she climaxes, she bites into his neck, and the blood spurts all over their bodies in an ecstatic release of two pleasures at once. That's exactly the point, I can finally see, as it's the union of the two opposites that makes the magic happen. You know. Yin and yang?

The Valkyries float down to hover above them, the two frozen gods of Hell, united in sperm and blood, and they begin singing Grieg's symphony, and my eunuch anthem, I suppose, "In the Hall of the Mountain King." I can feel the earth tremble as they sing, and the odor of Sulphur permeates the inside of this human skull. I hear again the tumultuous sounds of the bombs and missiles exploding and whistling through the night, all around the proxy war world.

Nearby, in Ukraine, where egos and heroes are created and soon collide on the cell phone and computer screens of salivating, flag-waving warmongers, humanity keeps its faith in the false myth of victorious conquest and that the ones who survive will be grateful to the leaders. Now I know that unless we can stop this guy's brother, Dr. Balder, the end of the world may take place.

One question still lurks inside what's left of my human mind: What if this is all being planned by Dr. Balder, and he wants us to believe we are fulfilling this ancient and historical prophesy? Don't all humans have faith that their leaders are telling them the truth?

Don't we all hope one side is better than the other and not a solid mass of evil, like the two joined figures I see before me, inside a giant, vibrating human skull? If all matter is energy, then Lily and I need to act.

When the Hall of the Mountain King explodes, I feel my mind blacking out, the same way I did on the Seal Beach Jetty, while being raped. The same way I did seeing the mounds of dead in Baghdad and the annihilated children, the mangled bodies never to rise again on the Earth. The same way Lily sees them.

The light from Lily's cabin is on, I can see, as I'm back inside my fifty-seven-year-old body again. She's opening her door, and she turns back toward me and smiles, wearing her powder blue business suit.

"Meet me here tomorrow, Martin. I know what we must do." She can speak again, and her eyes have that splendid, ice-blue gaze I have loved from the first moment I saw her photo online.

CHAPTER SIXTEEN: FIGHT FOR VALHALLA

September 2022, Utøya Island.

Now I'm back inside my troll identity, and we ride in her Volvo, out of Oslo, take the ferry to Utøya Island, and come to our destination of Valhalla Castle. Lily is ready to do battle, as the Catwoman persona of a giant Tabby, and the mystery of Dr. Balder and his spirit ghost and son, Loki, is fixated in our minds. I finally see that our fantasy physical forms are not seen by humans, as they simply smile at us and wave us through. It's as if a great barrier between us has been removed, and she and I are at last able to be who we were always meant to be. Lily is blasting the music of Led Zeppelin's "Immigrant" as we roll up to Dr. Balder's digs:

> *... will drive our ships to new lands*
> *To fight the horde, sing and cry*
> *Valhalla, I am coming!*

Inside this gnome suit, I feel like the same middle-aged, retired veteran and professor, but my eyes see my troll form. I can feel the stooped back, the leathery old skin, huge head, gray beard, and sagging jowls, not to mention my bulbous, clown-like nose. Lily explains that Dr. Balder and his cadre will see us as our transformed selves, and we shall see them as they become transformed to fight us.

I'm sad that we never had a real relationship over these long months. No breakfasts, dinners, or other meals to share our struggles. We were always separate—either because Lily was working on her cases--or she was out at her cabin in the woods, trying to discover what her secret Norse magical world was supposed to be. We ate on the run, inside hotels or fast-food joints, with Lily explaining nothing until that first day in March, when she changed me forever—inside and outside--at Troldhaugen woods, and later, when she took me to her rendezvous with Prince Hod in The Hall of the Mountain King.

"Mother? Is that you?" Lily is talking to herself. I wonder if it's Dr. Balder who's controlling her. She's now parking the Volvo in the lot below Valhalla Castle. I can see the dozens of Oslo and Interpol police cars parked next to the castle, with their flashing red and blue lights. True to his word, Dr. Balder has a special unit of Russia's Chechen troops marching back and forth in front of the castle. The cops and the troops are facing each other.

The news that morning says the police are not permitted to enter the premises because Dr. Balder, in his capacity as President and Chief Executive of Titan Energy, is holding secret meetings about negotiations with world oligarchs to stop the war in Ukraine. So much for the suspicious rumors of his having a den of iniquity inside the central portion of the castle.

When we're out of the car, I can see a blonde woman coming toward us down the hill from the castle. Catwoman Lily has frozen in her tracks, and she's murmuring to herself, or to her mother's ghost. I'm wondering how we'll be getting inside the castle to confront Dr. Balder, as I haven't seen a single Huldra or Huldrekall yet. I can't believe my eyes, as the woman approaches us. She is the living figure of Lily Orkidedatter, in her powder blue business suit!

I turn back toward Catwoman, and she thrusts the mistletoe arrow into my neck. The rush of adrenaline and drug overpowers my troll form and human spirit, and I sink to my knees. The last thing I see is Lily, or what I think is Lily, taking the arrow from the Catwoman's hands and pointing down at me. They are both turning into waving bodies before my eyes, but I can still hear them talking.

"Hod will be here shortly to take him inside. Good work, blood sister. I told you I would become you, and now I am. Dr. Balder has everything ready for you both. We'll go inside Valhalla the back way. We have the special QR codes, and these humans can't do anything to stop us."

When I come to, I am inside a stone structure. A room that is dark and wet, and I can smell mold and mildew. Rats scurry across the granite floor, as I rise to my feet, and my troll head is aching as if a sand blaster has been scraping the insides of it for eons. This must be the inside of Balder's castle. But where is Lily and, more importantly, *who* is Lily? Is she that Catwoman I was talking to, or the Lily duplicate who called her a blood sister? If the latter, it means she must be the serial killer, Ingunn Dahl. Lily was always telling me she was afraid of transforming into a killer. Maybe it's finally happened.

Something must be happening for them to bring me in here. My moron troll skin is still on, so somebody's controlling my appearance. I can hear commotion outside the metal door. Somebody's coming. Maybe the cops got approval to SWAT this place after all.

The door creaks slowly open, just as in all the other Gothic novels and movies. What's next? Bela Lugosi and Count Dracula? I vant to drink your blood! Wait! What are these ten characters filing into my prison cell? What the hell? Five of them look like young men dressed in pirate outfits. Each one is smoking a fatty joint. Rings in their ears, tattoos on their arms, and scars on their faces. But the faces are all green and covered with boils! Fork tongues are slithering out of their pointed, lizard mouths. Horrible freaks that stumble toward me, laughing, and waving their marijuana in the air, trailing streams of smoke.

The other five are soldiers. Dark, uniformed men in green, with full black beards. Holy shit! They wear the insignias of Saddam Hussein's personal guards. But they also have the lizard skin and the forked tongues.

All ten of them shuffle toward me, drooling and cackling, and that's when I feel my body moving. It's changing into something else! All matter is just form, to be changed by a higher will. A more powerful force!

I can smell the garlic odor of phosphorus and see its red glow all over these creatures. There's a putrid smell of spoiled meat, and I can see the rats forming a pack behind these ogres from my worst nightmare. I have become Martin, the twelve-year-old boy again.

In a panic reflex, I grab my ass cheeks and begin to cry, as the oncoming horde shuffles toward me. The dark cell is sweltering and smoky, and they circle me, like predator apes. Music begins to play, being broadcast by some hellish DJ somewhere inside the castle. Fleetwood Mac, singing from my childhood, when I was twelve. My rapists were playing it on the Seal Beach Jetty that night. "Don't Stop."

As they push me down to the floor, and rip off my jeans, I can hear this song inside my head: *Don't stop thinkin' about tomorrow!* All I can imagine, as I hear the zippers on their trousers open, is that it's not tomorrow. It's the eternal now!

The voice comes booming out of the speakers: *How do you like this, Dr. Pacifist?*

From above, I can see him inside his control room, where Marilyn and Olga were supposed to work. My daughter is correct. I was used by Balder and his son to addict her to his sex display businesses. She was nothing more than a gender toy for him, to see if he could sell his father's sex antics with Lily in a drama showing inside one of the Circle of Maldoror rooms. The police now believe Balder is here with his oligarch business friends and billionaires to discuss the war in Ukraine. What a lying scoundrel this ogre is!

And now, to add to his control, Balder is broadcasting her partner, Dr. Seagraves, as he is being raped by ten men inside a castle dungeon. What kind of depraved mind does this? I can't do anything but watch and listen to Balder rant on about his glorious plans for the future. To think that I brought them together and watched it myself makes me sick. I must now make amends. I will listen to them, and when they bring my daughter from her cell, I will act. These demons will not conquer Norway, much less the world!

"My son, how is the confrontation going between the Russian President's guards from Chechnya and the police? Were you able to stop Orkidedatter's Huldras from seducing the guards?"

Dr. Paul Balder, V, is wearing his finest Thor outfit, with his bronzed muscles and long blonde hair contrasting with the Asgardian Steel breast plate, inscribed with the sacred Runes of Odin. Odin once cast Thor down to Earth as punishment, but why does Balder identify with him?

Thor's battle armor helped protect his body while dealing with the curse of Hela, so perhaps he thinks he has been cast out of Valhalla also? Like the Christian Satan. No wonder he became Hodr to destroy Odin's Hall of the Mountain King by marrying my daughter when she was transformed as Hela.

Loki, the pale image of his idol, the poet Lautréamont, is encased inside his standing prison, his body's surface sparking like a huge, demented firefly, in the corner of the control room. To think I believed he was helping my daughter, instead of planning to murder those two young women, Marilyn and Olga, is quite insane.

"I cast a spell on those fairytale whores of the woods. They began to froth at the mouth and run around the Russian guards like springer spaniels, pawing the air, howling, and leaping like monkeys, until the Chechens began laughing."

His father bellows with Viking laughter until the computer monitors begin to rattle inside the walls.

"As for those giant black underground monsters, the Huldrekalls, they were even easier to restrain. You proved it with your white Huldrekall version at the first love tryst with Orkidedatter. All they wanted to do, after a love potion was administered, was fuck. Like goats, they chased after anything with a hole in it. Women, cats, dogs, donuts, Oslo and Interpol police. Of course, they could do nothing to the real world. Thus, they never made it into the castle to battle us or our demons."

"Is Ingunn Dahl still watching her?" Dr. Balder asks.

"Yes. I can feel them coming, down the castle corridor, around the Circle of Maldoror. They're here now." Loki points, as the door opens with the electronic password.

My daughter, as she told me, is the tabby cat. This Dahl serial killer has taken over her body. I wonder what kind of control this requires. I need to wait.

"Very strange indeed, Orkidedatter. I must say, you were much more alluring in your other forms as the Huldra and Hel, Goddess of the Underworld. I want to have a little fun with you, nonetheless. We shall turn things around again, and I shall be ... who? Let's see. From what we discovered in your past, you seem to be enamored of a certain lupus creature, no?"

How did he know? I didn't tell them anything. Astrid Lily shakes her head, and I can see her claws protrude menacingly. She leaps at her tall captor, but with one thrust of his right hand, a rocket of black light erupts from his palm, and hits her furry white chest, knocking her backward against the stone wall. She falls to the floor, gasping for breath.

"Please get it all into your twisted brain, Orkidedatter. My power comes from the very highest realm. Don't you understand the rules? Every country has a leadership that plays my game, not yours. The tighter the control, the more the rich at the top want kinkier and more exclusive enjoyment. Bigger and faster cars. More weapons and technologies to protect their riches. When their business becomes war and annihilation of the innocent, their minds get almost as twisted as ours. Isn't it wonderful? Perverts are wearing an 'M' on their backs because of me!" Dr. Balder waves his hand toward his son. "Loki, please switch them. I can't imagine fucking Ms. Dahl, no matter what she looks like. I am a spiritual man, after all, and it's what a woman is like on the inside that turns me on, as all educated and handsome men, like myself, believe."

"Yes, father, I want to see this performance as well! I have been without direct exposure to carnal mayhem for quite some time. Miss Dahl did allow me to enjoy her woman-on-woman bondage sex recently, before she killed her victims. Did you know that the vaginas on women will get wet even when their lives are in immediate danger? I did not know that. One learns new things every day."

The creepy pale boy inside the glass cage looks horrendous. His eyes glow behind a purple haze of demonic anger, and he points at my daughter's form and mumbles some gibberish chant. There's an electric discharge, and I see an exchange of black lightning between the cat and Lily's form. However, as soon as Ingunn Dahl occupies the cat's body, she morphs into her six-foot human body again, with the pock-marked face and her limp, dirty hair. She grins, showing her tobacco-stained teeth and long, vampire canines.

Lily stares at Dr. Balder as his body begins its metamorphosis. His broad, heaving chest and tall stature remain secure, as does the armor and wolfskin loincloth around his waist, but his arms grow thick, long hair, like black grass on the heath, under time-lapse photography. His muscular forearms and his bulging biceps also erupt into a hairy forest of fur.

Finally, his smiling lips and handsome blonde locks begin to blacken into pitch dark, and his eyes turn into riveting red bullets of lust. His human ears begin to grow out into a predator wolf's long and pointed variety, and his mouth and jaw extend slowly into a gray, whiskered snout, and his long fangs snap at her, as the sputum flies everywhere.

He sniffs at my daughter from across the room, raises his lupus head, and howls. The only part of his anatomy, I see, that remains human, is his long, fat snake of a penis, and it is slowly engorging with werewolf blood.

"Miss Dahl, please start the camera," Loki instructs, removing his trousers to get more comfortable. His skinny legs and boxers are quite incongruous. He reminds me of the young students I had to entertain as clients during my days in Oslo as a prostitute.

As the Wolfman Balder approaches my daughter, she is obviously unnerved and wary. But there seems to be an invisible attraction between them, as she retreats away from him. Some inner turmoil erupts, and her body begins to shake. She shrieks several short yelps of passion. Her legs become thinner, and so does her entire torso. Her thirty-eight-year-old facial features lose the crow's feet from the corners of her eyes, and her blonde hair glistens and the tinges of bleached faded strands disappear. Her ruby red and soft lips pucker into a youthful, plump, and impetuous pout. She raises her thick eyebrows and smiles at the Balder werewolf, who is now just a few steps from standing next to her fifteen-year-old body.

They are in suspended animation. The werewolf has taken my daughter's human body up into his arms. He carries her out the door of the control room. I follow in my spirit form. The physical surroundings move them. Their bodies no longer move. They are moved by a secret energy beyond time and space. I can see Lily's chest expand and contract with deep breathing. This must be an experience she has had before, perhaps in her dreams, but now it's being magnified with the dark reality of potential death at the hands this evil demon.

I wonder if I should insert myself in this picture. As I watch my daughter being dropped onto the velvety red bedspread, on the canopied four-poster bed inside Dr. Balder's suite, I can't help but think she is using him, and not the other way around. I know the truth of her powers, and I will therefore allow her this ironic thrill. What this entire situation deserves is the first love scene with Lily as a human, even if her paramour is a werewolf. A very rich and powerful werewolf.

Obviously, the human bedroom dialogue is non-existent, as my daughter is enthralled by the piercing red eyes of Balder's wolf persona, as he shucks off his breast armor, removes his loincloth and other clothing, and then leaps upon the bed, on all fours. He's above her, looking down at her illegal young body, and then he begins to lick her arms and legs, one by one, as if, under her suit, they're choice pieces of lamb.

I keep wondering about how many ribald versions of *Little Red Riding Hood* there are. This scene must be right up there with the most exotic and erotic. I can hear the squeaking wheels of a cart coming into the room, however, and it's Ingunn Dahl, the killer, pushing the electronic cage of Loki into the room. When she maneurvers Balder's son into a prime viewing position, she struts over to the digital camera controls on the wall and switches them on.

The wolf man removes Lily's powder blue business suit jacket, skirt, white blouse, bra, and panties and tosses them against the wall. He then uses his front teeth to scrape along her tattooed back, arms, and legs, his red tongue lolling out of the side of his black snout. His saliva drips on the red covers. as he gazes upon her nude body with satisfying pleasure.

Lily begins to moan almost immediately, under his power, and she rises to a seated position. She then encircles her hands around his bulging bicep and pulls him toward her. She stares at his human, twelve-inch penis, between his hairy legs, as he moves over her.

Sexual dalliance is a completely physical rush, no matter how much philosophical discussion is made about the internal spirit. Even Lily's partner, Dr. Seagraves, admits that the reason most religions are exponents of sexual purity and chastity is because they understand its need to control the animal in the human, and this "lust," which interferes with their control over their entire "flock."

I also understand how this control can change in a heartbeat. Now, Dr. Balder thinks he is controlling reality, no matter how dark and revolting it may be. But soon, as the story goes, the tables can turn, and "who is now first, shall later be last," and not necessarily in any future heaven, but right here on Middle Earth. My own experience, for example, with the werewolf Hans Wortle, is hardly romantic, but Wortle's stabbing may also turn into something different today. I will enjoy my daughter's bawdy reward, at any rate, and allow fate to create an existential irony of my own disaster.

I can't help but enjoy the fact that my daughter often tells us she is a villain and Dr. Balder is a villain. It is only Dr. Seagraves who places her on a pedestal by giving her an homage as the "good villain" of the evil arts and the folklore of our people. As I watch Astrid Lily writhe under the yearning and muscular body of this wolf man, I have my doubts about how "good" she really is.

The low growl of the werewolf man is vibrating the entire bedroom, as he slurps his red tongue between Lily's breasts, and her nipples become stiff red buttons. In an animal motion of flashing speed, as if he's catching two rabbits in two different holes, his snout goes from one nipple to the other, bobbing his dark head up and down, lapping, sucking, and nibbling at them until my daughter begins to command him like a dog.

"Faster, you brute! Take all my breast into your killer maw!"

At her order, he opens his mouth wider, and soon he has her entire breast inside his cavernous jaws, but he takes delicate care to never use his flashing teeth, to make her bleed, even though she, at one point, screams for him to do just that.

I fear her desperate need for blood comes from her childhood infatuation with abuse and maltreatment. The sex abusers in her orphan Oslo foster families, after her grandfather died, and her future fascination with the rapists who described their own fantasies to her with such libidinous, detailed gusto.

I hope I can eventually change all her need for torture that's stored inside her subconscious. She is obviously still under Balder's power right now, as he knows about the weaknesses from her past sexual exploitation.

The werewolf is now between Lily's legs, and she arches her waist up to allow him to lap thirstily at her vagina, as if drinking from a forest stream in midsummer. His strong and tan human hands, at the same time, reach up to knead her soft breasts, like a cat, until she begins to thrash beneath him and yell out.

"*Åh det er bra!*"

When she screams this, he starts to howl, and pushes his right fist deep inside her pink, virgin womb, as he rubs her clitoris with his left hand's thumb in a frantic, vibrating, back-and-forth motion. Her vagina spurts love juice all over his hand. Her long blonde strands of hair are lashing against the silk crimson pillowcase as her head whips, from side-to-side, in passionate ecstasy.

That's when the ugly one, Ingunn Dahl, turns on the music to give the couple some background sounds for their audience to enjoy during the climax. Appropriately enough, it's the British group, Duran Duran, and their pop tune "Hungry like the Wolf."

The beat of the pounding, jungle-hunting sound makes both Balder and Orkidedatter move into a frenzied overdrive on their bed of pagan desire. The werewolf creeps between Lily's legs and places his index finger gently between her labia, the little house of pleasure, and rubs, thrusting in and out until she groans in pleasure. He then increases the number of his digits and the vibration, and begins to lick, with his long, canine tongue, at the small dollop of her clit, the tiny cherry at the top of her passion sundae.

Balder the wolf is now at full mast below his waist, as he turns Lily on her stomach to give her what she craves most. He is, after all, part canine. He begins by slapping her buttocks with both hands, leaving red indentions on her two good and bad angel tattoos on each cheek. She screams again, "*Åh det er bra!*" and flashes a smile of devil's delight, behind her, as he strikes again.

His knees are dug into the bed like a bull, as he brings his throbbing red and engorged snake up to her dripping vagina. He slaps its huge pink hood upon her clit, beating out a rhythm to the words from Duran Duran, "I'm on the hunt. I'm after you." This is the moment he chooses to plunge his fat cock deep into her cunt.

What happens next, I cannot describe properly, as it becomes so fast and furious that humanity can't endure its ferocity. Lily and her spirit rival begin to howl together, as if the full moon were above them in the woods, urging them into an insane and thrusting locomotion of anger and fury against every human barrier to their lusting pleasure.

The semen that erupts from his penis sprays over her ass and onto her back, which is decorated with the tattoo of the naked and horned nymph, who smiles. Balder's cum spreads on the nymph's mouth, as she sips from her cup of green marijuana leaf, kneeling at the edge of the Oslo fjord.

Whew! I wish to blazes I could have a body to enjoy this right now.

CHAPTER SEVENTEEN: ANGRBODA'S REVENGE

I can see it is time for me to enter the picture. The reality of where my daughter gets her supernatural powers must be made clear to everyone, or she will remain under the obsessive control of Dr. Paul Balder, V, and his spirit son, Loki Balder, victim of the 2011 shooting on this island. Like Loki, I am a spiritual entity, which is simply a ghost, or what is left when the body has gone, and the soul cannot progress into another form. We can only converse with our fellow spirits or with our direct relatives from our life in this world.

Just as Astrid Lily Orkidedatter never became aware of her powers to shapeshift until she began to work with the miscreants and defective souls in her job with the police, so I was never aware of who I was, until I saw Dr. Balder and his serial killer monster, Ingunn Dahl, murder the two Huldras, Marilyn Southbine and Olga, her adoptive mother.

That fact is that both Dr. Balder and Lily Orkidedatter are different sides of the same Norse Folklore rivalry coin of the realm. Therefore, they easily gravitate toward one other and only a cataclysmic change in power can force them apart.

What I am about to show Lily will, once and for all, explain to her what her job will be in this world to come. I know she will not expect this, as she now believes I, the ghost of her prostitute mother, Ingrid, am her mother, and this is not true. I will now explain to them all what will happen, and why this day and future events were always meant to happen, from the beginning. I can feel my flesh and blood boiling, as I drift down from the rafters inside the Circle of Maldoror and into Dr. Balder's private love chamber.

Their bodies, his as the superior Werewolf Viking, and Lily's as the fifteen-year-old victim of his passionate control, are now resting in each other's arms. It's as if this is the moment between scenes in a play when the last act is about to be resolved. I feel a growing power of my own, as my actual form begins to take shape before them, so they will both finally see who they were meant to be, and why this is the turning point in all that came before.

As my body comes into focus, I can see Lily's physique change back into her thirty-eight-year-old woman's form, and Dr. Balder changes back into his blonde businessman's body. His megalomaniac's body. Both stare at me, wide-eyed and in shock, as I point at them, accusingly, and with vindictive anger.

In the mirror next to where serial killer Ingunn Dahl stands, and the large cage for Loki Balder sparks and crackles with dark purple current, my body becomes solid and displays who I really was on that day when Lily's grandfather killed the fox and held it up to the window for her to see when she was a young girl on the farm.

The most beautiful woman in the world, the Goddess of Fertility, and Queen of the Valkyries, appears in the mirror before me, and all the others stare at me in wonderment. I have long, flowing red hair, an angelic face that beams with moonglow, and my soft yellow gown, with fringes of spring flowers, is ephemeral, so my breasts and legs show through.

I must admit, I am in a state of shock. If I am Freya, in my spirit identity, then who was I in my human life? Wasn't I the Oslo prostitute who was stabbed to death by the psychopath, Hans Wortle? Those are the only memories I have.

This change must have happened when Lily's grandfather murdered those two prostitutes. Could it be that Lily and I were both changed and cursed that day? If I gave birth to Lily, then she must also be somebody else in the Vanir clan of goddesses.

It's Dr. Balder who has read my mind because he steps forward, a wide grin on his handsome face. He taps three times on his silver armor breast plate before he speaks.

"You, as Freya? My, my, so what will you do to us now? Fuck us to death? Where are your two kitties to take you places on your chariot? Or is that what you use? Maybe it's the magic cloak of falcon feathers. Is this what gave you the ability to fly around like Tinkerbell? I can see why your daughter became a cat. Another weakling in the Norse pantheon."

I can feel the full power of love and passion flow into me as he says these things. This must be why I am the most powerful goddess of them all. I control all the fertility in the universe. I spread my arms out wide, as it is now time to discover who my daughter really is, and what happened on that day on her grandfather's farm.

The cage of Loki Balder starts to vibrate. I have only known him as Dr. Balder's evil son, who lied to me about his father giving my daughter sexual pleasure, but he is now changing into someone quite different. In fact, his metamorphosis is accompanied by a holographic display into the past right inside the same cage.

As the door to the big enclosure swings open, we all stare at the show as the scene opens on the farm of Sebastian, Lily's murderous grandfather. It is 1990. Loki's body has transformed, from the pale, homely body of the French poet of the macabre, Isidore Lucien Ducasse, into the tall, muscular, and virile shape of Odin's court jester, Loki, the dark-haired warrior, and supreme trickster.

Is this a trick by Balder? According to legend, Loki was the one to murder Balder by tricking his blind brother Hodr, whom my daughter met and made love with at the wedding inside the Hall of the Mountain King. She killed Hodr and destroyed the place, and that's why she later obtained the mistletoe. However, Ingunn Dahl, using Lily's body image, stole the arrow Lily the cat was going to use to kill him, and now Loki is showing us the history of how my daughter Lily, and I, came to be who we are today.

Loki is also the god of fire, so it's no surprise, after he steps out of his cage, that he crosses his breast plate armor with his muscular right arm, and an orange flame explodes to life in his palm. He strolls over to Lily and hands her this flame, and her body instantly ignites. She doesn't burn or scream. She just stares, serenely, inside this roaring infernal halo.

At the same time, her grandfather from the past is raising his arm to point at his five-year-old granddaughter. A bolt of fire from his finger crashes through the window, while Lily's eyes are fixed upon the dead fox in Sebastian's other hand. My daughter's body is also engulfed in flames, and I know who I am, and who she is.

I am the witch and prostitute Sebastian murdered that night. Her memories are now filling my brain like a creeping virus. I understand what is on display inside this cage. The Loki inside this room, in 2022, also stands, in 1990, right behind Sebastian in the dark. Loki is smiling, his hand on the old man's shoulder, as Loki shapeshifts into the second prostitute.

Loki of legend can change sexes, as part of his bag of tricks, and I see that I was the first prostitute, who later became the fox, after Sebastian stabbed me seventeen times. I can feel its vixen red fur on my body now. That night, my identity as Ingrid the Oslo prostitute and Lily's mother, was created, by Loki's curse. He never wanted me to see my identity, especially my inner spirit self, Freya.

The light into the past goes out, in a puff of purple smoke.

Loki the warrior sheds his wolf cape, his steel armor, his leather boots, and now stands naked inside his father's bed chamber of passion. In a rebellious act of extreme bravado, Loki points his index finger at Dr. Balder, and a purple bolt of lightning strikes his father's forehead, freezing him on the spot. As Loki struts toward my daughter, his long penis dangles between his hairy legs, and I can see what this means.

Igunn Dahl turns on the background music. It's the Jimi Hendrix Experience and "Purple Haze."

Balder, the brother of Hodr, cannot move to stop this Loki from grasping Lily by her bare, flaming shoulders, and kissing her deeply. The roaring fire subsides, giving way to a new, carnal flame of desire. This is the mating foretold in Norse legend between Loki and his bride, the giantess and Goddess of War, Angrboda, my Lily's inner spirit. After this lovemaking, I know, Lily will be growing very fast.

Despite the importance of this activity to the confrontation we are having against Dr. Balder and his Valhalla Castle, his thug woman, Ingunn Dahl, has the presence of mind to start the camera to sell the sex to the wealthy, worldwide subscribers inside the Circle of Maldoror. When Lily pushes Loki against the wall, and grabs his big cock in her right hand, I know their fire may ignite once more, but it doesn't. Loki bites her neck and yells a Viking charge, "*Videre til seier!*"

She has his entire penis inside her slurping mouth, spitting saliva up and down the shaft, swirling her tongue on his pink penis helmet, as the tall dark god of tricks moans in ecstatic pleasure. She grabs his balls with her other hand and twirls them as if they're a sack of gold coins, rubbing the shaft, up and down furiously, and bringing her vagina up to his long, hairy, and strong legs to press her pussy against them and squirm.

They spin and twirl their bodies and angle toward the giant crimson love bed. When they're finally supine, the trickster decides to switch gender! He is now a tall brunette female, with purple lips and eyeshadow, large breasts, hard round nipples, brown areolas, and her pussy has been shaved like a baby's behind.

Lily doesn't seem to mind, as her tongue continues to dive, inside the labia's lips, swirling her long pink serpent against the bulb of the woman's clit until the Loki woman also screams, "*Videre til seier*!" Now their bodies *do* ignite into flames of passion once more! Their torsos burn, like Roman candles, the skin on their bodies crackling under the heat, the smoke erupting into clouds of purple steam.

And yet, just as quickly, the fire is out, and Loki's balls and penis grow out again in his garden of pubis. He is back to being a man, and Lily is twice as empowered with lust, as she smothers his hard cock with her wet vagina and begins to ride it, her thighs squeezing it so hard I can see her anus pucker, and the two angel tattoos on her butt cheeks dance. I have never seen such a powerful, driving force between two mating adults. The bed shakes and moves, as in the *Exorcist*, to the pulsations of the thrusts, squishing "thwaps" of suction, and pounding rhythms of sexual intercourse on a god-like level of excellence.

When the climax comes, there is no sound. It's as if the world stands still. I am too wet myself, and I want to fling my body upon them both to experience their shivering, joyous orgasms. But when she has finished, Lily pushes him off, as she remembers that Loki is from the dark side of the pantheon. He is forever the monstrous joker, the son of Dr. Balder and his world sex-trafficking ring, so she sits up, and slowly, like a woman crawling from the heat of the desert into a shady portion, an oasis in the corner of the gigantic bed, Lily begins to grow.

Her stomach is engorged already. It is filled with something large and squirming beneath her skin. "*Herregud*!" She is pregnant with his offspring already! Her belly expands at such a furious rate of speed that I fear she will burst. However, as if her body is prepared for this, her torso begins to swell and grow on the bed to meet the expansion of her pregnancy.

In only ten minutes, her body is huge. She is a giant woman, over fifteen feet tall, her legs curled beneath her swollen stomach until she must stand to become ready for what's next. Just as her sisters, the Huldras can do, she is going to immediately deliver what's inside her bloated stomach onto the floor of the castle's room. Her body has changed into the Goddess of War and the dark phantom of the North, Angrboda! She stands upright and delivers the first of her triplets in a slow gush of blood, skin, bone, and royal blue placenta.

I know who they will be, as it is foretold in ancient Norse legend.

The wolf Fenrir, the Midgard serpent Jörmungand, and the ruler of the dead, Hel. Lily has already taken on the body of Hel that Balder created for her, but this new Hel will be hers alone. Hel will be on our side to fight the demons of Valhalla Castle. The trafficking evils of sin and corruption we will battle against forever, until only one side will survive.

We watch her three children grow to giant proportions, and when they are over ten feet long, standing next to their mother, who has taken on her full armor of the Goddess of War, with the flowing blonde hair under the steel helmet, I can see the Vanir clan symbol inside the circle on her warrior breast plate. Her face is dark and forbidding, as she frowns across at Dr. Balder, and then waves her spear at him. She knows there can be no end to this castle's satanic business until he and his demons are defeated in a fair fight to the end.

When Balder again comes alive, his son, Loki changes, back into the spirit son who was murdered on July 22, 2011. A pale, morose being, who slinks back inside his cage and shuts the door. His father, however, has other plans. He raises his powerful arms and bellows with all his might so that all the demons in his castle can hear him.

"Begin the reign of terror on these weak creatures of sorrow and delusion. These human sympathizers, who wish to destroy me and my world of pleasure, will become flowing fountains of blood from which we can drink, until we are satiated by their cowardly hearts of unreasoned compassion! We shall grow even more powerful, more resolute, and more victorious than any gods who have ever fought!"

We hear the demonic cackling of Balder's psychotic monsters, and I know where he's harvested them. They are the rapists, murderers, and dark monsters from my daughter Lily's human job on Earth as a psychotherapist for the Oslo police. His powers extend to the darkest side of life, into the raving souls that have given my poor daughter nightmares for all these years, until today, when we must fight her demons to the death and save the last hope for humanity and its future.

Before this begins, the door to the bedroom opens, and it is an eight-foot-tall monster troll with the human face of the raped and abused Dr. Martin Seagraves. He has, by Lily's magic, been released from the dungeon to come and assist us in this fight to the death.

Martin's huge, hairy head and long, pointed ears are flushed red with passion and hate. His bulbous nose and face are beaten and scarred, dripping with blood. He opens his gaping mouth and snarls, his sharp teeth snapping like a bear trap, as he pounds his huge fists against his monster chest of armor. He finally begins to roar out his love for his new employer, the Queen of the Northern Dark Night. Angrboda, the Furious redeemer of lost souls.

After my second rape experience, I am a changed man. Just as Lily has been manipulated and forced into her sex experiences, so have they done this to me. I am bloody, scarred, my asshole feels like a line of Russian tanks has plowed through my colon, but I am bigger now, and I am ready to fight with Lily Orkidedatter and her mother to retain our dignity and our freedom to love whomever we wish to love, without control and without force. But before I wage all-out war, I want to tell this reprobate why I am fighting him. It's not just for Lily or for me. It's for all those abused and controlled people, hiding in plain sight, who never get recompense for the damage done to their minds and souls.

I raise my long, troll arm to get Dr. Balder's attention. He smiles at me and looks amused, but he nods for me to speak. Thank you for small favors.

"The reason you and all you represent will be defeated today is because you are a plague upon the entire world, not just in Norway. I am from San Diego, and my experience of being raped was traumatic, yes, and you knew this, so you used it against me. This goes on every day, however, as people get labeled and shoved into a corner to be ignored or packed into some special interest group that becomes irrelevant. You keep up a false front of philanthropy and environmental awareness while, secretly, you harbor the most sinister sex trafficking business in the world."

Dr. Balder raises his arm. "Pleasure is not illegal trafficking in anything. All my clients are legally doing what they enjoy doing, in our private domain, and their utmost privacy is protected. War is legal and not private at all. Rape and many other atrocities occur during war, with no repercussions, unless one side eventually loses, and then there might be trials."

"Quiet! You phony, lying bastard! I know about laws that protect the abusers. You have your law to mark molesters, but you just want to profit from it with your technology. It's always the enforcement of law that makes it work, and your enforcement is about to come to an end. If we can do it, we will fight you in court to stop your private sex swinger parties for parents and guardians. Why? Because pedophiles attend and fish out victims. Gangs and pimps use children to run drugs and to serve as prostitutes, and you think it's all good business because they come from poor families, or they are simply learning about the real world, as you call it. You are not from the real world, as we now know, and neither are we, so we can fight you here, where you live in secret, hiding with your Norse mythological identity. Lily Orkidedatter and her mother are now more powerful than you because they represent freedom from oppression—both psychic and physical. They have changed me, also, and now I know why I must fight. Get ready for your punishment, Balder!"

After Dr. Balder gives his little shout-out, and Lily changes into the Norse War Goddess, Angrboda, things become very different, as you may well imagine. No erotic sex. No images of lust and sex slavery for profit. Just boring violence on a spiritual war level. Spiritual war? Haven't you ever thought about that? That there are wars going on inside your mental existence (what the ancients call the "soul")?

That's what we're doing as Norse creatures. Warring with our spiritual identities. Yes, we can die, but only at the hands of other spirit identities. There are two levels of combat. One in the "real world," and one in the "spirit world." It is Lily Orkidedatter who gives me her magic to become part of this other war. So, be patient, as I describe the action from my limited perspective. I'm no omniscient god here, you know! Just a lot bigger and nastier troll with a bad attitude. The way they taught me to be in the U. S. military bootcamp for officers. No more mister nice guy pacifist on this spiritual plane!

What I think might be a problem, the bunch of rich assholes who are enjoying themselves in the different castle rooms inside the Circle of Maldoror, proves to be non-existent. In fact, the entire ruse of Balder discussing a possible end to the war in Ukraine is fictional. What is real is the fact that Balder is streaming all the tortures and sex activities going on to all his paid subscribers around the world. Yes, my own rape is included, which embarrasses me to no end, because Balder's magic forced my body to go back to my twelve-year-old self again. I guess his clients enjoy the rape of a boy more than a fifty-seven-year-old wrinkled professor and veteran. Who can blame them? I do.

As for our immediate foes inside Balder's love chambers, namely the entrepreneur wizard himself and his tricky son, Loki, they can see the size of Angrboda's three kids, Hel, the Goddess of the Underworld, Fenrir, the huge wolf, and Jörmungandr, the coiled serpent, so they decide to transform into the rats they really are and leave the room through holes they must have drilled beforehand. That leaves female serial killer, and Lily Orkidedatter look-alike, Ingunn Dahl.

Sadly, as with all folks with souls and minds of pure evil, she decides to fight it out, as the noise of Balder's other minions, Lily's police work pedophiles, murderers, and criminally insane psychotics, can be heard as they pour into the castle. As I was plagued by my former child rapists and Saddam Hussein's elite guards, Lily is also having to fight her own demons from the past. This is what we all do, after all, once we can clearly see the dark shadows of our past that make up our existence.

At fifteen feet tall, Lily, as her spirit identity of Angrboda, makes short work of the serial killer and bedroom DJ. She grabs her by the top of her grimy head and lifts her, screaming, off the floor, and quickly runs the spear through the imposter's mouth. The spearhead comes out the back of the woman's skull like a human shish kabob. In fact, the giantess stares at the head, as it comes clean off the shoulders of the woman, and she spits in Dahl's face.

"You don't look like Lily," she says, smiling. "You are much too ugly!"

Angrboda then flicks the skull off the spearhead, like a green martini olive with a stuffed pimento, and her black wolf child, Fenrir, raises his great head and opens his huge mouth to grab it, like a dog catching his master's thrown ball. His razor-sharp teeth crunch down on Ingunn's head, swallows it whole, and licks his chops.

Angrboda looks over at me. "You know, I also didn't care much for her choice in music. As for the sex, what can I say? Not my choice in men, but it was my first romp in the hay as a human in over four years. It was also necessary for my transition into the real me. It's nice to know I can now go back to real men if I choose." She lifts her head and roars, at the top of her voice. "Let's exterminate the rest of the vermin inside this putrid castle! The sooner we do it, the sooner we can return to the woods and my cabin!"

I don't know if I like the new-look Lily. The old one ignores me, but this one frightens me. She seems to have a constant chip on her armored shoulder. However, I guess it comes with the territory. I also want to get some pay-back for my experience in the dungeon, so I follow her and her three "kids" out the door of the love chamber. The sound of the cackling, insane monsters from Lily's past is deafening as we step out into the dark tunnels of the Circle of Maldoror.

CHAPTER EIGHTEEN: EXTERMINATION OF DEMONS

Following Lily as her revengeful spirit self, Angrboda, I can finally see her true nature. She is a loving, caring, sensitive woman who needs to be appreciated for who she is and not controlled by her dark, passionate senses, which was what Dr. Balder was doing all along. Just the way society controls us by its forceful manipulation of our emotions, so was this completely evil and dark manipulator trying to control Lily with sex. He is now, therefore, suffering the consequences of what my grandmother called "pulling the tail of the tiger one too many times."

In fact, the differences between Balder and what he represents and what my Lily represents go much deeper. As I'm the intellectual of our group, unless that wolf and snake can talk, let me preface our violent confrontation with a copy of the poem Lily wrote just before we came to this castle. It says what I will discuss in a much better way than I ever can:

SEDUCTION'S JEWEL
I let you seduce me between red tulips and the blue creek.
My moan is so quiet, only my warm breath can be felt on your neck.
Tender fingers are on the right place.
He is smooth with his tongue all over my body.
He keeps me dancing, yearning, and sucking.
He kisses me like there's no twilight tomorrow.
He whispers to me like there's no sunlight to catch.
He grips my hips with his strong arms like I'll never have another orgasm.
He licks, swirls, presses, and pulls me down on the green grass.
I throw my head back and he removes my hair from my face to watch my joy.
I can't stop squirming.
I ride him like a bull when the dusk is knocking on the gate to heavenly pearls.
The stars blush and the moon is jealous while you

make love to me inside the creamy milk from my Orchid.

Shoot your seed down my hallway, let's make the world bigger tonight!

Let the sky witness us when I carve your name on the top of my pumping heart.

I'm the jewel's dewdrop you don't want to let fall...

I am eager to lick the white liquid off as you lie beside me under the moonlight's torch.

Now, dear reader, if you would. Please contrast this poem's content with what took place in the previous chapter in the "love scene" between Lily and Loki, Dr. Balder's spirit son in the form of the Norse god. This poem tells us what Lily Orkidedatter believes to be the inner desire she feels with the one she freely chooses to be her lover. This is the subjective love that can be seen as going beyond the physical carnality of Loki and Balder and into a place where it is the individual lover who determines what is passionate and worthy to embrace. When Lily has sex with Loki, she is controlled by Balder's lustful idea of what the sex act is to be enjoyed. Lily has no choice about fucking him, if she wishes to become what she is right now, the warrior goddess, Angrboda.

However, Lily is not Angrboda inside her brain. She is a woman who wants the freedom to love a man of her own choosing. She wants the freedom to communicate her needs, her hopes, and her fears to this man and to expect a rational, hopefully unbiased response. This belief, in fact, if you read it symbolically, which I, as a literature professor do, means that the imagery she uses can be taken on both a literal and a figurative level.

For example, the "jewel" in the poem can be a physical jewel of some kind, or, most importantly, it can be the symbolic jewel only she can allow to "drop," which gives her alone all power and control. It means "seduction" can take place at any age, no matter what the person looks like, no matter who the person chooses to love, and no matter where the place she chooses to be passionate is located, according to how they care for each other. The most important ingredient, in my opinion, is Lily's ultimate freedom to say "when and how" she feels about the act itself.

I can hear you, and your Dr. Whiffenpoof's Song. Oh, let's all sing together of the ways true kindness and compassion will overcome power and the forceful will of the human mind!

As we move into the hallway of the Circle of Maldoror, this voice is coming at us from the walls. The only person it can be is Dr. Balder, in his rat body, scuttling in the darkness across the putrid rocks inside this palace of sin. What is his trick now? My partner's transformation into the Goddess of War has subjected him and his son into groveling vermin, and yet this twisted mind of his goes on.

"Is that you, Balder? Your victim, Astrid Lily Orkidedatter, is free of you. Why do you insist on plaguing us with your games? For your information, I have changed also. We have both been released from your personal curses as the Wizard of Pure Evil."

When I look at Lily, up ahead, the confident expression of warrior Angrboda has disappeared. Her spirit self is also known as the "bringer of sorrow." Her face, in the flickering torchlight, is drawn into a scowl, and her huge body lurches, in furtive lunges, all around the narrow, circular hallway, as the sound of this demon's voice reverberates inside our ears.

This voice sounds squeaky, like a rodent, and yet it fills with gusto, at intervals, as if the inner demon can overpower the gray, furry body. Can he truly be getting into her psyche, even now, after she's fully changed into a warring giantess from the Ironwood Forest?

Oh, my poor orphan, Lily! All your decrepit past has again returned to assail you. Did you believe you could escape it? Did you believe in this idiot American coward's claptrap? Did you believe your grandfather was simply a common murderer of two prostitutes? How do you think you became a medium and a counselor to insane monsters? Why are you, of all women, worthy of fucking the supreme evil in the universe? Because you were a respectable child, commendable of the best this spirit world has to offer? Oh, no, Lily. Your soul, my daughter, is now in the hell you created for yourself!

As my Lily shows more fear on her face, her children show more panicked anger. I imagine they want to protect their spirit mother, in her obvious state of vulnerability, as I do. Jörmungandr, the snake, slithers his stretched purple body along the crevices at the base of the hallway's walls, trying to find a hole to enter, hoping to get at Balder and his son, Loki.

Fenrir, her black wolf, is growling deeply, frantically sniffing with his snout everywhere and hopping up on the wall to howl. Lily must pet him to make him calm down.

Finally, Hela, the half-dead woman, is chittering insanely, pounding on the walls with her fists. Her tattooed body, slithering tongue, and whipping bat tail move constantly, in rhythm with each word he says.

Let me first get the progeny issue out of the way. Yes, your mother was the witch and prostitute your grandfather killed on his farm. Yes, she does have the spirit identity of that pussycat of love, Freya. No wonder you like cats! However, my lass, this is when your heritage gets strange. As a humanitarian for profit, and a grand master of our Earth's energies, I employ only those who can obey me and reflect my ingenious power over others. Your grandfather was one such man. He was a wizard of pornography and murder, were you aware, Lily? He first served the Third Reich during their occupation of Norway in World War Two. He supplied them with young girls with whom they could frolic, and he also did some freelance curses on that King of yours and his stupid followers in the Norwegian resistance.

"I never saw him do that! You're lying. My grandfather was kind to me. He only killed those prostitutes because they were trying to rob him. He showed me the dead fox of her body!" Lily's voice is high-pitched and frightened, as if she isn't quite certain about what she says.

Oh please! I thought you were a psychologist. Aren't you aware of how the mind represses those experiences too horrible to remember? Your kindly grandfather, Sebastian, first experimented on you. He knew children were ideal for high paying clients who wanted to have youngsters to play with them, so he played with you and ... what do you call it in the shrink profession? Grooming? Ah, that's it. He groomed you, Lily. You became his first young tart to sell to the highest bidder. Under my supreme auspices, of course! As we know now, our spirits stay the same, from one life to another. We simply change our bodies to fit our purposes, as your friend Dr. Seagraves so wisely informed you. Until the final battle, we must continue to take on new worldly bodies to fight.

Like many politicians and the superrich these days, we don't know whether to believe him or not. With this added layer of Norse legend and monsters, the present becomes a bit of a conundrum, to say the least. No matter what happens, I will stick by my Lily to the end. Faith is, indeed, much more powerful than belief.

"Whether you are lying or not, Balder, it makes no difference. Let me know what your game is, and what you plan to do right now. Dr. Seagraves has taught me the importance of being present and allowing the past to become merely a wake at the stern of my human body, constantly fading from view and never interfering with my important actions in the now."

There is a deathly silence within the walls of Valhalla Castle. The dripping of water can be heard along the circular passageway, and Fenrir is growling, as he creeps along in attack position, his black belly grazing the cobblestones, and his ears flattened on the sides of his huge head. We are coming to the first of the rooms used for private sex and other deviant activities. It has an oval door frame made of Norway Maple and a glass cut-out at the top.

I creep up to the door, squat down, press my heavy stomach against it, and I peer inside.

Oh, Dr. Troll wants to play my game! How fun! I believe you were snooping around other journalists and discovered about my interest in the new "M is for a Pure Society" law. What's inside this first room proves my case about needing a defense against such predators loose on the streets of the world. What are the rules? You and your collection of Norse freaks must enter these rooms and defeat whomever you discover in there.

"What do we win if we clean-out the room of your monsters, or whatever you have inside there?"

Did you also know that I want to dissolve the crown in Norway and make it into a republic governed by an independent chancellor, elected by the people? Did you realize it is I who will run for this new position? Dr. Seagraves, do you recall how a certain German politician, for whom Lily's Grandfather Sebastian worked during the second world war, was able to gain his power?

"He ordered his Black Shirts to blow up and set fire to the German Parliament, the Berlin Reichstag, on February 27, 1933."

Oh, Lily! You do have a smart partner! Correct again. If you should be defeated in any of these rooms, then my little fire inside the home of the Crown Prince at Skaugum in Asker, west of Oslo, can be accomplished. I've been there many times, and I've made a carefully crafted layout of the palace. However, since my main objective is to bring about the fight for complete domination of the world at Ragnarök, on a very spiritual level of existence, I must play by these antiquated rules.

This means that I can't set-off my firebombs until you are defeated here. And I can't allow President Putin to intervene either, as he has nothing to do with our fateful meeting, except in a very peripheral way. Putin has, of course, endorsed my efforts. He will support me once I become the new leader of Norway.

Lily has regained her composure. "Once we do our housekeeping in your castle, then what happens to you and your pervert son, Loki?" Her voice again sounds confident.

Do you think I'm stupid enough to give away my ending to you ghastly failures? You, who are just entering the playing field of spirit battles? Just open that door, and if you survive, open the three others. Then we shall see what happens, shall we?

What I love about my experience in the natural world is that it is predictable, up to a point. If I schedule something, then as long as I am healthy, and there are no intervening transportation problems, then I can usually perform with confidence. It's as the ancient Stoic philosopher, and former slave, Epictetus, stated, "We don't control what happens to us, we can't control what the people around us say or do, and we can't even fully control our own bodies, which get damaged and sick and ultimately die without regard for our preferences."

This new experience as a spiritual being who can die, however, is the most frightening reality I've ever felt. Even if my spirit does become born again, in another life, events like my second rape experience isn't exactly what I see as enjoying spiritual bliss in any life. In fact, it makes the Iraq War seem like a college football game. Since I now know we're fighting toward the end of the world, I suppose, being on Lily's side does make my chances appear somewhat favorable.

As Lily opens the door to the cell, I follow directly behind her. I clutch my spear with both hands and try to see inside the pitch-darkness, to no avail. Balder is obviously making things as difficult as possible for us. In fact, I can hear the skittering of tiny feet inside the wall. The odor in this room is sulphureous, damp, and putrid. It's like being inside an enclosed entrapment where hundreds of people have died over time.

The shape comes into view in the center of this circular room that looks to be over one hundred feet in circumference. This demon is pulsating a vivid red glow, making the room appear like the inside of a cheap brothel, but it's the outer form of this beast which paralyzes me in place. My eyes rivet upon it the way I gazed upon the dead children bombed by our missiles in Baghdad. I am not disgusted in my soul the way I was then, however. Rather, I am appalled this ogre is even displayed. Even Hela, who is half-dead, is cringing away from this demon. The purple snake winds around Lily Angrboda's legs, and her wolf is whining next to her.

What can I say to describe it? It is a huge form, almost twenty feet wide. It's a perfect rectangular shape, with the four sides at the required three hundred and sixty degrees total, with no hint of being human, except for the front section of its body. This section has grasping hands of all shapes, sizes, and colors, that are grabbing at the air desperately, as if it can fulfill something inside its geometry if it could only reach it. The skin on the rectangle is horribly pock-marked with boils, lesions and scars, and the smell of these rotting fissures is disgusting.

A most horrific mouth is in the direct center of the front of this rectangle's body. It's about three feet in diameter with a long, wide, pink tongue, filled with white tastebuds. The tongue also keeps exploring the air, making a smacking sound against the lips as it does so. No eyes. No visible means of smell. But the revolving and revolting satellites of penises and vaginas, also of all shapes, colors, and sizes, with and without pubic hair, are the strangest part of this beast's physical appearance. They encircle its rectangular center in at least a hundred different orbits.

I surprise myself by saying the first words. As I did in the war, I try to be funny. "Anybody you recognize, Lily? Perhaps it can think outside the box."

"Silence! I am the totem of all the demons of desire you never controlled, Lily Orkidedatter. You simply wrote poems about us, as pathetic individuals, or you laughed with the police, and put us away with the other masturbating and narcissistic souls within your psychiatric wards and prisons all over the world. We often pretend to be sane, and are released, or we escape. Or we grow alone, in any type of family, and we became wealthy and famous. We are today billionaires, leaders, and warriors, and we thrive in every sector of society. This will not be a test of your physical power, but of your intelligence. If you can defeat me in a debate, then you have won this cell's prize."

"Why don't you be silent? You are a deformity of human emotions!" Lily is shouting, and she startles me out of my miasmic haze. "I have never been in love. I have been in lust, you foolish icon. I am awakening to my own sensibilities, and the most important sense to me is my intuition as to what I need to become a total human being. What is your debate topic? Can it have anything to do with your own pleasure principle, by any chance?" She laughs.

"Who will judge this debate?" I ask. I do not understand the rules of these battles between spirits.

I shall!

A new, powerful voice causes the castle to rumble and quake as if the Earth itself has been moved from its axis.

"Who are y … you?" My voice is shaky and feeble.

The one who oversees all your activities, of course. Even though I gave my eye to achieve my magic and wisdom, I will listen to your answers, see their details, and then I shall read the Book of Runes to see which of your answers is the best for all the world's peoples. Remember that I have access to all historical wisdom. A poor answer will be lost from history, never to be seen again. And whomever will be victorious in all four rooms shall be protected by Thor, my son, in your future endeavors!

"Oh God! I mean, Odin. I hope your mind is up for this, Lily," I whisper to her, placing a hand on her muscular shoulder. I see that even though she's occupying the spirit body of Angrboda, she still has the same tattoos my partner Lily has, which I believe is a good omen.

What allows humanity to achieve the greatest glory? Power or love? You must give your reasons for the answer you give, or you will be disqualified. You, the storehouse of hidden passion, must respond first. You may both give two supporting responses, but no more than this shall you give.

The mouth of the rectangle opens to speak once again.

The greatest glory goes to the ones who have the most powerful weapons to subdue the enemy. Women want the alpha males to protect them and their children, and what better glory can there be than to lord it over your own land and people, and keep the invader out with your strength and laws that give you the best control? From the first moment a human picked up a weapon, it was seen that ever more advanced weapons meant ever more powerful control. Once controlled, love and adoration can flow like milk and honey from the people who are tamed and protected, achieving a balance forever. Power is the most important possession to achieve any human glory!

He may well have been reading out of any textbook given to officers in military schools. Even though words may change, such as transforming from a Department of War to one of Defense, the current philosophy of the most powerful nations is that of a war on terror itself, and that means having the freedom to attack even before being invaded. This requires the most powerful weapons ever devised. I am afraid my Lily has little chance at defeating this monster's argument.

Angrboda Lily moves to the center of the room and spreads her arms out wide. She looks up into the darkness of the rafters as if seeing through the castle's infrastructure into the limitless sky above.

Without love, there can be no chance for power to exist at all. We are not created by some superior force from above. We grow out of love for our land and our own people. When two people agree to procreate, or adopt, it is the most powerful moment in human existence. Certainly, we must protect that freedom to love, and we must also educate those who grow out of that love for one another. If we are always controlled by weapons, how can that be glorious? Without a chance to find other ways of living together, without powerful weapons, how can humanity advance at all? Love brings about birth and new life, and it cannot end in death by the strongest overlord. What greater glory is there than to allow love to grow freely in our humanity's mind and hearts? Only love breeds trust and through trust grows a natural protection that withstands all disasters.

We don't need to hear Odin's pronouncement or rationale about who won the debate. We see the result. The demon of lust begins to expand. Slowly, the rectangle grows larger, ballooning out from the center until the mouth is a gaping maw, the tongue lolling out of the side. Then, all the obscene and orbiting penises and vaginas burst, one by one, until finally his entire form explodes, and is obliterated into dust. The stench in the cell is replaced with an odor of spring jasmine, and neon butterflies appear out of nowhere to fill the room's darkness with light.

So much for the demons of Lily's past mistakes.

We hear the scurrying vermin feet inside the walls, however, and we know there are three more cells to conquer. The oval door swings wide, and we file out of our first trial and into the Circle of Maldoror. Before we go on to the next cell, I want to find out how Lily was able to find that answer so quickly. I grab her arm and she turns around to look at me. She is a medium, and we had our affinity from the beginning, when I was living thousands of miles apart in San Diego.

"Lily, my dear. How did you come up with that superb response?"

She takes a deep, soul-wrenching breath and then blows it out, as if she were making all her past disappear in that one exhale.

"When Dr. Balder told me about my grandfather raping me, I was so traumatized by that information I instantly remembered it happening. It shook something loose inside me. When he molested me, I had an out of body experience, and I ran outside, into the woods. It was night, the moon was full, and I felt the wind and the rain hitting my body with full force. Blood was running down my legs from his penetrations, but all I could see and hear was my heart beating. I then saw it all so clearly, and I began to cry with joy. What I saw that night was what I spoke just now. That I was part of everything, and everything was love and perfect, even when it was evil and dark. The floodlight view of taking in all of it at once was like looking at the bottom of an intricate rug, with all the twists, pulls, and mistakes. That's the rest of life, outside my personal spotlight view of life. And I knew we all have these little apertures of lonely existence. But this single floodlight of love shines through all our pinpoints, even the animals, spirits, and monsters. I know this light is perfect love, but we can't see its grandeur unless we understand that all the twists of darkness, and what we call evil, must also exist to make it all perfect. That's all, Dr. Seagraves. That's what I know now."

As she speaks, she shows no emotion. I begin to cry, however, as this wisdom is what I am also searching for in my life. I blow out my breath and march behind her, resolutely affirmed that nothing is going to stop us now, no matter what is behind those three final cell doors.

CHAPTER NINETEEN: LILY'S METAMORPHOSIS

October 2022, Lily's Cabin in the Woods

Lily Orkidedatter, my hero, is sitting with me outside her cabin and watching the snow come down on the tree canopy in front of us. With the Rondane Mountains in the distance, I keep thinking about when she allowed me to watch her, in her Balder-induced Hela form, making love to Hod in the Hall of the Mountain King. That other person was not the Lily I sit with today. In fact, after she told me inside Balder's castle about when she was a little girl on the farm with her abusive grandfather, and the way we cleaned house of those demons inside the last three castle cells, I knew she accomplished her heroism with love and not hate.

I don't look at her, and she doesn't look at me. We both stare with fascinated attention at the small, floating snowflakes falling all over the Earth. It's as if after all these months of living in the lusting and controlled world of Dr. Paul Balder, V, we can finally see who we are for the first time.

"Lily, you made me understand something about life that I had refused to see until that night inside Valhalla Castle."

"Oh, yes? That you can head-butt three of your rapist demons with one blow, while my children Fenrir and Jörmungandr calmly devour the other five, and then eat your three for dessert?" She smiles.

"Not exactly. Even though I have fallen off the pacifist wagon. After I saw you use your martial arts of love inside those final three rooms, you showed me how strong love can be, girl! I love the way you talk to your victims. 'That was a wonderful bite, Mr. Wolfman! You need to aim for flesh next time. I'm afraid you're going to need a partial plate for those magnificent canines.' I almost fell on top your black wolf I was laughing so hard!"

Lily finally does turn to look at me. Her ice-blue Viking eyes are the clearest I've seen them in nine months. Her police duties are now scaled back because Dr. Balder's castle was burnt to the ground when Lily's horde of Huldrekalls and Huldras burst onto the scene and started dancing through the Circle of Maldoror with torches, lighting up all those rooms of debauchery. The Oslo local police and Interpol officers also ran Putin's special detachment of Chechen guards out of town.

"I learned so much from you, Dr. Seagraves. Aren't you excited to be able stay on in Norway to work with me? I promise to keep my libido in proper perspective now that I have discovered my true inner self."

I take her two hands into mine. "Yes, but what about Dr. Balder and his son, Loki? After we defeated his demons, Odin spoke and said he could do nothing about Balder's life as an entrepreneur or as a continuing wizard of evil. Odin, in fact, changed them both back into their former identities. Doesn't that make you change your mind about how we work together? How can I help you now? The only spirit powers I can get must come directly from you."

"This is what I want to tell you. With Thor on our spirit side, the fact that Dr. Balder can still run for political office is a big threat. His M for Purity Law is still in effect, and he plans to run on a conservative campaign to keep the streets of Norway clean of lowlife and degenerates."

"I see. There was no evidence to pin on him after the big fire destroyed it all. I suppose my suggestion about giving so much freedom to your Huldras and Huldrekals didn't work out very well. They burnt down all our evidence with their free spirits!" I laugh half-heartedly.

"It was our word against his, and we certainly couldn't tell them about fighting Balder on a spirit level like the Matrix. I have a difficult time getting them to believe I can talk to dead victims. That reminds me. I have some bad news to tell you after all."

Astrid Lily Orkidedatter's downcast eyes tell me a lot. This must be some very bad news. "Go ahead, my dear. Do you want to marry Thor and rule the world on your own? Can I be his manservant Troll, at least?"

"No. That's not it. I still have a dark soul, Martin, and what happened to me inside the castle proves what my destiny must become. And, I must admit, I rather enjoy the idea. I want you to help me accomplish my plan."

She stands up and takes off her powder blue business jacket. Her eyes become radiant in front of the snowy backdrop of the woods. When the rest of her clothing drops to the ground, without her body inside, I panic. I fall to my knees and search inside her clothing. When the black widow spider jumps on my knee, with Lily's head on its cephalothorax form, I am not afraid. Even her eight ice-blue eyes don't frighten me. She rocks back-and-forth on her the eight spindly legs, and the bulbous, shiny-black abdomen, with the infamous orange hourglass on the bottom, gives me a curious feeling of comfort, believe it or not. If she's going to become a Spiderwoman, I'm all for it.

I don't even shout when she speaks to me.

"Martin, this is my own idea. I was bitten inside the castle by one of these, just as I was turning into the spirit identity I wanted to become for my next case. The concept is to become a vampire who can infiltrate Dr. Balder's businesses and dens of iniquity. I can also enjoy my sexual and blood appetites, the dark nature of my real loving soul."

"Why are you now a spider? What happened to you?" I reach down to pet her head, which still has her blonde hair, albeit in a diminutive coiffure. The sun has now gone down outside in the woods, and when Lily's spider body grows into a tall, statuesque blonde woman, in front of my eyes, I step back away from her.

She is the blonde equivalent of a vampire, with large, firm breasts, an hourglass body that must be in her twenties, which is encapsulated inside a long, sheer black evening gown with two long slits up the sides, exposing her lusciously tattooed legs with Lily's large Orchids etched upon them.

"*Herregud*! How can this happen? Do all the Dracula rules apply here? Can you live forever if you get your victims' blood? If so, what about your spider form? You don't become a bat to fly around at night? Do you at least have to sleep inside a coffin during the day? I can't think straight. Tell me, Lily!"

She strides over to me and gently touches my pulsing neck, with her alabaster fingers and long, blood-red fingernails. When she leans into me in the darkness and smiles, those two pear-white, vampire fangs appear inside her open mouth, and I lurch backward despite myself.

She throws back her head and laughs uproariously.

"Oh, Martin! Don't you see how much fun it will be? Instead of the boring bat persona, I will become a poisonous black widow spider during my travels, until the sun goes down. Seeing the world from that viewpoint will be exciting. Danger everywhere I go, but I can transform, when needed, into my human vampire form. I can keep my spider poison and web weaponry intact! Dr. Balder's human billionaire friends from around the world won't be able to resist my beauty and charm! I can't stop thinking of all the fun and games I'll have with the web bondage, blood sucking, and, of course, using my spider's poisonous venom!"

"I see. Some fun. How can I assist you? Also, what about Dr. Balder and Loki? Can you attack them in this form? At least when you became Angrboda, you gave birth to your three little helpmates, and you turned Dr. Balder and his son into rats. What about now?"

"That's the bad news. I wasn't in control of this. The spider was sent by Balder's magic, so I can't attack him as a vampire or a spider. But I can go after him where it hurts. His sex-trafficking businesses and his campaign to become the new chancellor of Norway and usurp our Crown Prince. You can help me defend against any demons he might send our way now that you've gained your own powers. Odin said I can give you an upgrade."

After saying this, Lily waves her hand over my body and says something in Norwegian. It must be a vampire or witch's curse, because my body becomes the young, tall, muscular, and blonde hero from The Hall of the Mountain King, complete with my own hammer. I am Thor! I hope she isn't infringing upon any copyrights. Nah. Not with the ancient legend of Norway and Scandinavia. My spirit identity is in the Public Domain. I am good to go! The greatest thing for me is that I'm no longer fifty-seven years old. I am young, powerful, and dynamic. I'm an alpha and not an epsilon. Now. If Lily can only turn on the music of Grieg inside her cabin, we can play around a little bit here.

Just as I lunge toward her, to embrace her against my broad armored chest, and hold her in my chiseled, ripped, and powerful arms, she breaks away from me, laughing like a schoolgirl. Before she leaves, she waves at me again, and I return to my old, retired professor's form.

"I need to find my own true love now, Martin. I am free at last to love as I see fit! Please won't you turn on the TV so we can watch *Charlie's Angels* when I return?"

I stand on the front doorstep to her cabin watching her fly through the forest, her web silk spinning out of her boobs, as she sails over the treetops and into the night. She looks rather like the woman I grew up watching on TV, Elvira, Mistress of the Dark. Wait. Isn't she gay? Oh well. So much for my fantasy life. I hope I can turn on her old TV. I wonder if she keeps any popcorn. Glad I brought my overnight bag from the Navy. Maybe she'll read me a story so I can fall asleep faster. Those fangs did nothing for my self-confidence, I can tell you that! Oh, my Lily, you're so beautiful and yet so independent.

Before she returned, I wrote the following poem about two orchids I saw in the woods that day. They reminded me so much of my love for her. I wrote it inside the diary she kept under the bed.

ORCHID LOVE

Her skin, soft and white, growing amid the forest moss.
I love to back out of her fragrance, for she leaves her stigma
All over me. Sticky with dew and pollinated blood.

I am trapped by her imagination.
The craving and feeding of herself
Only orchids can do this. Alone, passionate, desire.

Until the union of us all, she stigmatizes for darkness
Flowering energy of being kept in her hothouse.
Ivory legs splayed, the petals of memories beyond time.

In my hypnotized daze of love, I creep onto her silky waves
Transfixed motion, pollinating overflow onto me
Until I burst from confusion and dark hate.

She keeps feeding herself from my body,
A female wild Jesus in the tomb of a forest primeval.
I can't cut her, keep her, or grow her on my own!
Only the insects can have her, creeping inside,
Sucking the stigma of eternal wetness,
Sapping the strength of old and young men,
Until they are all blinded forever at her altar of sin.

THE BLACK ORCHID

There will be a lot more comedy in the second urban fantasy in the Fire Eyes series. *The Black Orchid* will star Lily Orkidedatter and her sidekick from America, Dr. Martin Seagraves.

Plot synopsis:

Dr. Paul Balder, V, and his spirit son Loki placed a curse on Lily at the end of book 1 *Orkidedatter (Orchid Daughter)*. She must remain a hybrid black widow vampire until the curse can be broken. Therefore, she travels around the world to "vamp" world leaders and billionaire members of Dr. Balder's secret society of evil doers.

Lily will have her new mascot, a snow-white Italian Volpino (fox) named "Ozzy" (after rock legend Ozzy Osbourne). Seagraves hates the dog and thinks he's trying to become the oldest dog on record, beating out the 21-year-old Mexican Chihuahua.

As she has her hot sex, Dr. Seagraves will be envious, as Lily continues to resist his romantic advances. Seagraves does, however, make appearances to protect her as a "hammerhead" version of Thor, which he does with absurdly comedic effect.

The Black Orchid will be a romping excursion around the world for Lily and Martin and her "little dog." Castles, billionaire mansions, oligarch yachts in the Mediterranean, will be scenes of hot sex and bloody "bites." Just what Lilly loves!

Ozzy

Free Sample from *Orkidedatter* read by award-winning narrator, Nikki Delgado

Go to emrepublishing.com

Free Sex and Intimacy Audiobook Course Taught Online by
Psychotherapist Lily Orkidedeatter
and Professor James Musgrave
Enquire at emrepublishing.com

This course* is a private discussion by students and hosts about why sensuality, sexual intercourse, and what one does with his/her private body may be of no concern to anybody but the private person. And, if society does have a stake in what we do, how is this regulated and applied? Certainly, a "one size fits all agenda" usually doesn't work. So, how do we compromise? Perhaps it's how each person establishes personal boundaries and awareness concerning how our sensual beings are manipulated and used by others for profit, for personal power, and for many other reasons other than what is good for the individual. What we enjoy in the way of sensual and sexual stimulation is up to us to determine, within reason, and that will be the "theme" of this course. We will also discuss societal rules about this, as they differ by what the separate country and societal laws say. Who is right? Who is wrong? Why do we have these boundaries, and what good do they do for humanity?

On the book's launch in mid-July, there will be other free gifts awarded (bookmarks, keychains, signed paper copies), so stay subscribed to this newsletter for more info. Thanks for your support for this worthy cause, and please report any sex abuse you experience or see to authorities using the RAINN network of authorities.

James Musgrave and Lily Orkidedatter

ABOUT THE AUTHORS

Lily Orkidedatter has been a medium and educated psychotherapist in her job in Oslo, Norway, for over twenty years. She's also working for the police to question victims, witnesses, and accused psychopaths, pedophiles, rapists, and killers. The poetry included in these novels are from the haunting, true-life events she's lived. She decided to lend her identity to award-winning author, James Musgrave. He's crafting this series. Both Orkidedatter and Musgrave are childhood survivors of rape and sexual/mental abuse.

To see Lily's list of current books of poetry and artwork go to: https://linktr.ee/Orkidedatter

James Musgrave is a childhood rape survivor, U. S. Naval Veteran, and award-winning author of over forty fiction and non-fiction titles. He works for the V.A.'s suicide-prevention hotline and counsels and sponsors recovering addicts. All his historical mysteries have been vetted and accepted by the American Library Association's Biblioboard.com program for sales and distribution. He was also a journalist and English Professor for over twenty-five years in San Diego.

—Se cuidarme. —Por primera vez en todo el día, la chica sonríe para después, volver a centrar su atención en la bestia y, ante el asombro del vampiro y del tuzhandés, se lanza al ataque contra la criatura nocturna, empuñando sus dos espadas, mientras recita a toda velocidad un viejo hechizo, que encadena a monstruo al suelo durante el tiempo suficiente para que ellos dos huyan del lugar a lomos de sus respectivas monturas.

—¿Puedes decirme qué es lo que has hecho con él?

—Nada, nos hemos librado de él, y es lo que verdaderamente importa.

El sonido del agua cercana llega hasta ellos, y la chica pica espuelas a su caballo, que acelera y se planta en poco tiempo en la orilla del lago, en cuyo centro emerge la pequeña isla de Thanaria, destino de la joven aventurera.

—¡Thanaria!

—¿Cómo llegaremos? —Ulbrin no tarda en llegar a la orilla y agudiza su mirada para observar